Hexed

Allen Sircy

Published by Southern Ghost Stories, Gallatin, Tennessee

ISBN: 979-8-9988146-3-1

Table of Contents

Prologue

The man's name was Arthur Pembrook, and he believed he was cursed.

For two years, his hardware store on Market Square had been slowly bleeding out. The business his father had built, the pride of his life, was being choked to death by a new, bigger store that had opened just two blocks away. Every customer he lost felt like a personal wound, every unpaid bill a fresh line etched on his face. He prayed. He took out loans. He did everything a good, God-fearing businessman was supposed to do, and none of it had worked.

Which is why, on a moonless Tuesday night in 1947, Arthur Pembrook found himself standing in the dark, silent alley behind his own store, clutching a dusty Mason jar. Inside was the concoction the young black man in the North Central apartment had prescribed to revitalize his business: a strange, murky mixture of citronella oil, vanilla, and wintergreen, all muddled in the gray, dirty water from his mop bucket, with a handful of mustard seed settled at the bottom.

It felt like foolishness. It smelled like desperation.

With a furtive glance down the empty street, he began to walk the perimeter of his store, sprinkling a thin, dark line of the liquid across the threshold of the front door and beneath each of the large display windows.

He stood there for a long time in the quiet darkness, the empty jar hanging from his hand. He didn't know if he had just performed a blessing or committed a sin. All he knew was that he had finally done *something*.

Two nights later, a mysterious fire gutted his competitor's warehouse, ruining their entire stock. One month after that, Arthur Pembrook hired two new employees to help him with his flourishing business. And like so many others in Knoxville with secrets in their hearts, he knew he owed it all to the strange, quiet power of Obie Lee Roddie.

Just a Dab

The stairs creaked in rhythm with her footsteps, a staccato beat up the spine of the old apartment building on North Central Street. It was 1948, and Knoxville buzzed in the low thrum of postwar energy—trolleys rattling past tobacco shops, newsboys calling headlines about Truman and strikes, dogs barking at nothing in particular. But up here, at the top of the narrow stairwell, there was a different kind of noise. The thick, pulsing silence of expectation. Of secrets.

Mrs. Delphine Tucker reached the landing, one gloved hand gripping the wooden railing. She paused, took a breath, and smoothed her hat—dark velvet with a small purple plume, something just shy of fashionable. She wasn't here for style. She was here for help.

A gentle knock. Then a second.

The door opened without a word.

Inside stood Obie Lee Roddie—Dr. Roddie to those who dared speak his name in need or desperation. He was tall and dark-skinned, and despite the gravity of his title, surprisingly young—twenty-six—with a face that seemed always amused, always watching. He wore a white shirt, sleeves rolled, and smelled faintly of tobacco.

"Mrs. Tucker," he said, his voice a low, smooth baritone with a slight, melodic accent that suggested a home much farther south than Tennessee. "You're right on time."

She stepped inside, clutching her purse. The apartment's front room was simple and tidy, with a worn couch against one wall and a small radio humming softly in the corner. She followed Dr. Roddie down a short hallway to a beaded curtain. He held it aside for her.

As she stepped through, the air changed. It grew thicker, warmer, and was filled with the scents of sweet oil, tobacco, and something more primal—earthy, bitter, like dirt soaked in vinegar. This was the conjure room. A table sat near the wall, covered in little bottles, dried roots, feathers, and folded bits of paper. There were candles—some lit, some spent—and what looked like a beef tongue wrapped in string, resting in a tin pan by the window.

Delphine didn't ask questions. She knew better. As she entered, she caught movement behind her.

A light-skinned African American woman appeared in the doorway, drying her hands with a dish towel. She looked to be in her early 30s, dressed in a floral house dress and soft slippers. Her hair was wrapped in a burgundy scarf, and her expression was gentle, calm, and knowing.

Dr. Roddie followed Delphine's glance.

"Oh—this here's my wife," he said, smiling. "Lizzie."

Lizzie offered a polite smile and gave the towel one last twist between her fingers.

"Please excuse me," she said warmly. "Didn't mean to intrude."

Her voice was smooth, with the soft drawl of someone raised to speak gently, no matter the occasion. She gave Delphine a slight nod, stepping back and disappearing behind the thin curtain of beaded strands. As she passed through, the beads chimed faintly like distant wind chimes.

"She don't sit in on sessions," Roddie explained with a half-smile. "But she keeps this place settled. Prays over the pots, lights the first candle each morning."

Delphine returned the smile, though a touch of unease clung to her breath. She didn't know what she expected—some crooked old conjure man in a black hat maybe—but not this soft-spoken couple in a tidy apartment.

Dr. Roddie sat at the table. "Shall we?"

Delphine hesitated only for a second. In the corner she noticed candles lining a small altar. A faded Bible rested open beside a cup of water, beneath which a folded handkerchief was pressed flat. A paper with names, barely legible, sat beneath a brick.

He motioned for her to sit. She did, sinking into a worn red chair that gave a low groan.

"You have a name for me?" he asked.

She pulled a folded piece of paper and placed it in his hand.

Dr. Roddie reached for a small, round tin and set it beside a jar of sweet oil. He unfolded the paper with the name and pressed it flat with two fingers.

Delphine sat up a little straighter, the weight of the room pressing her words out slow.

"It ain't for me," she said. "My husband, Joe and I have been married for ten years. It's for my sister." Roddie didn't respond—he simply studied her troubled face.

"Her name's Glenda," Delphine continued. "She's thirty now. Works over at the shoe factory. Real pretty girl. Soft-spoken. Loves children."

Roddie nodded as he poured oil onto the paper.

"She's been courtin' this man named Willis Greene," Delphine added. "He's thirty-four. Owns his own car. Works at Brookside Mills. Two years they been courtin'."

"And he won't marry her?" Roddie asked. Delphine exhaled.

"Not even close. Every time somebody brings up marriage, he scoffs—like it's a joke. She asked him 'bout startin' a family and he laughed, said kids were too loud and too expensive. Said he ain't the type to be tied down."

Roddie's fingers stopped moving. He leaned back in his chair, long legs stretching slightly, and rested his hands on his thighs. His head tilted just a bit.

"Two years," he repeated, mostly to himself.

"She's gettin' anxious," Delphine said. "Glenda's real gentle, but this has started to wear her down. She's talkin' like maybe she ain't meant for a husband, or children neither."

"You believe she loves this man?" Roddie asked.

"I do. But I think mostly she's afraid," Delphine said, voice quieter now. "Afraid the window's closin'. Afraid she's gonna be just like my Auntie Myrtle. She died waitin' on a man who never came back from the war."

Roddie looked at her a long moment. Then, with a deep breath, he stood and crossed to the far shelf. He pulled down a blue bottle and a small pouch tied with twine.

"I believe I can help your sister," he said.

Delphine blinked. "You do?"

"I do," he replied. "But she'll have to do her part too. This ain't no spell you sit still for. She's got to wake up every morning and say she's worthy of a husband. Say it like a promise."

He set the pouch on the table.

"This here's a mixture for her. Tell her to sprinkle it under her pillow. Only at night, only when she's alone. And this oil—" He held up the blue bottle. "She should wear it behind her ears any time she knows she'll be near him. Just a dab."

Delphine reached out with trembling fingers and took the items.

"If he's got any softness in him," Roddie said, "this'll show it. And if he don't... well, she'll know that too."

He smiled—not kindly, but knowingly.

"There's no spell stronger than the truth," he added.

In the kitchen, the faint clang of a spoon tapping the edge of a pot reminded Delphine she wasn't alone in this space, but that whatever was happening here was accepted, even blessed.

She slipped the bottle and pouch into her purse, feeling heavier and lighter all at once.

"Thank you," she said softly.

Roddie gave her a nod. "Tell her the moon's in the right place for this. But it won't stay there forever."

Delphine nodded, clutching the items tightly in her purse. She stood, smoothing her dress. "How much do I owe you, Dr. Roddie?"

He offered a polite smile. "Fifty dollars, if you please."

"Of course," she said, not hesitating for a moment. She reached into her purse and pulled out a crisp fifty-dollar bill, placing it in his hand.

"Thank you, Mrs. Tucker," he said, sliding the bill neatly into his pocket.

Delphine turned to leave, passing through the

beaded curtain into the hallway. Just as her hand found the doorknob, she paused—there it was: a faint, persistent melody seeping through the wall from the apartment above. A piano, played with passion. Some church hymn, maybe. Or maybe just noise.

She glanced back.

Dr. Roddie stood in the center of the hallway behind her, still as a statue—except for his jaw, which had tensed. His eyes had narrowed just slightly. The music wasn't loud, but it was enough to draw a flicker of annoyance across his otherwise calm face.

Then it was gone. The smile returned, smooth as ever.

Delphine stepped outside, a new sense of hope making her steps quicken. She couldn't wait to get to Glenda's house to tell her everything and show her the instructions from Dr. Roddie. She was sure, it would work.

It's About the Piano

The faint chiming of the beaded curtain was the only sound as Dr. Roddie re-entered the conjure room, but the placid energy Delphine Tucker had left behind was gone. Already undone by the jaunty clatter of the piano overhead, Roddie walked straight to the altar and placed the fifty-dollar bill into a cigar box. After scribbling the amount into a ledger, he passed through the beaded curtain and into the kitchen, the floorboards groaning under his heavy steps. The lingering scent of sweet oil gave way to the aroma of simmering collard greens and Lizzie's rosewater hand soap.

Lizzie stood at the stove, stirring the pot with a long wooden spoon. She glanced over her shoulder, her calm expression faltering as she took in the scowl etched onto her husband's face.

"What's wrong, Obie?" she asked, her voice as smooth as river stone.

"It's him," Roddie grumbled, pulling a chair out from the small kitchen table with a scrape of wood against linoleum. "Playing that damn piano again."

Lizzie paused her stirring. She tilted her head, listening. The music was barely a whisper in the kitchen, muffled by walls and the bubbling of the pot. "You can't even hardly hear it in here."

"I can hear it," he muttered. "I've got Mrs. Gable in an hour, and I can't focus with that racket banging around my skull." He stood abruptly, his chair rocking on its back legs. "I'm going up there."

Lizzie turned fully, wiping her hands on her apron. Alarm softened her features. "Obie, don't. You'll just make it worse. They're renters, same as us. Let the landlord handle it."

"The landlord ain't the one trying to tend to people," he countered. He was already at the kitchen door, his jaw set. Lizzie reached out, her hand hovering near his arm before falling away. She knew that look. It was the same one that meant he had already decided the outcome.

He didn't stomp up the stairs as he wanted to. Instead, he took them with a controlled, deliberate pace, the sound of the piano growing louder with each step. It was a clunky rendition of "When the Saints Go Marching In," played with more enthusiasm than skill. He knocked on the door, twice, just as Delphine had on his own.

The woman who answered was Alberta Jefferson. She was a petite woman, somewhere in her mid-40s, though she carried herself with the rigid certainty of someone much older. Her hair was pinned in a neat bun that emphasized the stern set of her mouth. She wore a simple, high-collared dress, and her posture was ramrod straight, as if she were perpetually resisting the urge to slouch into sin. "Mr. Roddie," she said, her voice crisp and cool. She did not smile.

He forced one onto his own face, a practiced, charming expression that had eased the minds of a hundred anxious clients. "Good afternoon, Mrs. Jefferson. I do apologize for the bother."

The piano stuttered to a halt mid-hymn, like a bird startled off a wire.

"I was just hoping to have a word about the music," Roddie continued politely. "You see, I have patients I'm tending to downstairs, and the noise…"

Alberta raised a single, perfectly sculpted eyebrow.

"*Patients*?" The word dripped with suspicion, as though he had just confessed to running a gambling den.

A man's voice called from inside. "Who is it, honey?"

Alex Jefferson appeared behind his wife, a glass of water in one hand, his other resting lightly on the shoulder of a young boy seated at the piano. The boy's legs barely reached the pedals, and his fingers hovered over the keys with hesitant discipline.

Alex was the opposite of Alberta. A man in his early 50s and slightly overweight, he moved not with her rigid posture but with the relaxed, easy slouch of a man made of molasses. He had a wide, easy grin that bloomed the moment he saw Roddie at the door.

"Well, hello there, neighbor," Alex said in his warm baritone. "Nice to see you."

Roddie inclined his head, calm but purposeful. "And you, Mr. Jefferson. I don't mean to interrupt your afternoon."

"No interruption," Alex said, though he glanced back at the boy on the bench. "Just in the middle of a lesson."

"I understand," Roddie said. "I just needed a moment. It's about the piano. I know you've got a passion for it, and the music's fine, but it does carry downstairs. I've got clients—patients—who need a quiet space for their consultations."

Alex blinked, clearly caught off guard. He looked to the piano, then back at Roddie.

"Well now," he said, tone still affable but more measured, "I had no idea it was carryin' that much. Sorry 'bout that."

He glanced at the boy, who stared at the adults

with wide, confused eyes.

"We're almost done with the lesson. Just a few more scales to run through. If it's all right with you, I'll finish up, and then we'll ease off the keys for a while."

Roddie gave a curt nod. "Appreciated."

"Least I can do," Alex said. "I'll keep it in mind moving forward."

Alberta hadn't said a word since answering the door. Her eyes hadn't left Roddie's face, sharp and quiet, taking in everything.

Roddie met her gaze for just a second longer than necessary, then stepped back into the hall.

While her husband was all easy charm and apology, Alberta's gaze remained sharp and calculating. She hadn't said another word, but her silence was a statement in itself. She watched Roddie with the kind of intense scrutiny reserved for a moth flittering too close to a flame, her disapproval a palpable force in the small doorway.

Roddie met her stare for a brief moment before turning to leave. As he did, he offered her a small, knowing smile, a slight upward turn of his lips that was meant to be polite but landed as a private challenge.

He turned and descended the stairs, the sound of the Jeffersons' door clicking shut behind him. Downstairs, the apartment was quiet again.

As he entered, Lizzie stuck her head out of the kitchen, her expression worried. He offered her a confident smile and a quick thumbs up to signal that the matter had been handled. She smiled back, relieved, as he slipped behind the beaded curtain into his conjure room.

The immediate problem had been solved with civility and a simple request. But as Roddie stood in the quiet of his workspace, the lingering image in his mind wasn't Alex's agreeable face, but Alberta's cold, suspicious eyes. The music had stopped—but in its place, a quieter, more dangerous chord had begun to hum.

Neckties

Edna Gable climbed the stairs with the composure of a woman used to turning heads. She was dressed in a pale blue skirt suit, her heels clicking steadily against the steps. Her hat was white with a silk ribbon and a small veil that barely shadowed the sorrow in her eyes.

Roddie opened the door before she could knock twice. He stepped aside without a word, ushering her in with a tilt of his head and a soft smile.

She followed him through the hallway and into the conjure room. The space didn't intimidate her—neither the altar nor the strange charms in the corners. But her movements were slower than usual.

Lizzie Roddie gave her a kind nod from the hallway. "Make yourself comfortable, sweetheart." Then she vanished behind the beaded curtain.

Roddie motioned to a chair at the table. "What troubles you, Mrs. Gable?"

Edna sat, straight-backed and still.

"It's Douglas," she said, almost before the words had shape. "My husband."

Roddie waited. He knew when silence did more work than questions.

"He works at the real estate office down on Gay Street. Has for years. Always worked long hours. But last week, he didn't come home 'til midnight. Said he was in a meeting. When he came home, I could smell it. Whiskey and perfume."

Her voice cracked, but she didn't look away.

"I asked him straight out," she continued. "And he gave me that look. You know the one. Like I was the fool for even askin'. Like I oughta be grateful he came home at all."

Roddie's expression darkened, his jaw tightening. He reached over and grabbed a black notebook and began flipping through it until he came to a page titled **REVENGE**. "If it's revenge you want," he said, pointing to the paper with some faded scribbling on it, "you take some rusty nails and drive them into the ground around your house—just a few drops of his blood on each is all you need."

He paused, his eyes locked on hers.

"That's all it takes."

Tears welled in her eyes, but she shook her head.

"I don't want harm to come to anyone, Dr. Roddie," she said, her voice trembling. "I don't want to lose him. I just want him to see me again. Like he used to. Before the nights got longer and the lies started comin' easier."

Roddie's voice was soft when he spoke. "Mrs. Gable, may I ask—do you still love him?"

"I do," she said, her chin trembling. "I don't know why some days, but I do."

Roddie nodded slowly, then turned back through the notebook until he came to a page titled **INFATUATION**. He moved to a cabinet, opened a drawer, pulled out a small glass vial, then returned with deliberate steps.

"You got access to his closet?" he asked.

Edna blinked. "Course I do. Why?"

"You're gonna take one of his neckties," he said. "Doesn't matter which one, but it has to be something he's worn before. Sprinkle some of this on it. Then you take it, and you wrap it around your leg. High up. Under your skirt. Tie it tight, but not enough to cut off your blood. Then you go about your day while he's at work—cooking, cleaning, walking the dog, whatever it is you do."

Edna stared, blinking fast.

"As long as that tie stays wrapped around your leg," he continued, "he'll feel it. Like a pull he can't name. He'll be drawn to you. Won't be able to think about any woman but you. He might not even know why. But he'll come back."

The first tear finally slipped down her cheek. Roddie handed her a handkerchief, clean and pressed.

His brow crinkled.

"He ever put hands on you?" he asked.

"No," she whispered. "Just… just broke my heart a little, is all."

"Then let's try to put it back together," he said. "That's what you want?"

She nodded slowly, pressing the handkerchief to the corner of her eye. Then she stood, smoothing her skirt with trembling hands.

Roddie cleared his throat, gently. "Umm… Mrs. Gable, my fee for this service is seventy dollars."

She didn't flinch. With practiced grace, she opened her purse and pulled out a folded billfold. From it, she counted out the money—three twenties, a ten, and a crumpled single.

She placed it in his open palm without a word.

Roddie gave her a slight nod—equal parts gratitude and acknowledgment. There was no ceremony to it. No receipt. Just an understanding exchanged in silence, the way some prayers never leave a person's lips but still reach their intended ear.

♦♦♦♦♦♦

A little while later, Edna Gable stepped out into the late afternoon light, her purse clutched tightly in both hands. Her composure had mostly returned, but her cheeks still carried the faint red of recent tears. She didn't expect to see anyone on the stairs, so she was surprised when Alberta Jefferson came up from the floor below just as she reached the landing outside Dr. Roddie's apartment.

They nearly bumped into each other.

"Oh! Excuse me," Alberta said, stiffly. "Edna?"

Edna offered a tight smile. "Oh my, Alberta. It's nice to see you."

"It has been a long time."

There was a pause—just long enough for Alberta to take in the tailored clothes, the red-rimmed eyes, the scent of lavender and something older, maybe lemon oil or rosewater. She tilted her head slightly.

"You all right, dear?" she asked, her voice laced with curiosity behind its politeness.

Edna hesitated, not accustomed to sharing her troubles on a stairwell. "Just a bit weary, is all. Thank you for asking."

"Of course," Alberta said softly. "I live just upstairs."

Edna had no idea.

"I hope you don't think I'm being too forward, but I couldn't help but notice you were visiting with Mr. Roddie."

Edna's posture straightened slightly. She wasn't ashamed. "I was," she confirmed. "I had to see the doctor about my husband."

Alberta raised an eyebrow. "Mr. Roddie?"

Edna gave a faint nod. "Yes. the doctor. He listens better than most. And he don't judge."

"I take it your husband's … unwell?"

"He's under a lot of pressure at work," Edna said. "Long nights. Whiskey. It's.. it's really been hard on us lately."

Alberta clucked her tongue. "That's a shame."

"It is," Edna replied. She looked at Alberta then, trying to shift the sad subject. "Are you still married to Alex?"

A warmth bloomed on Alberta's face, and she glowed with a quiet pride. "Yes," she said. "He's a good man. I'm blessed."

Edna's smile this time was genuine. "I'm so glad to hear that."

They stood in silence for a beat. Then Alberta folded her arms.

"Well," she said, "I'll pray for you. And for him too."

"Thank you, I'll take all the prayers I can get.

"You stop by the apartment sometime soon, you hear?" Alberta said, her tone softening slightly. "We can have some tea and catch up properly."

A look of pleasant surprise crossed Edna's face. "I'd like that very much, Alberta. Thank you."

She offered a final nod, "It was nice to see you again," then turned and descended the remaining stairs, her footsteps soft and deliberate.

Alberta remained on the landing a moment longer, staring at the closed door down the hall.

She had never seen a woman leave Roddie's apartment quite like that—undone, but dignified. And something else, too: resolved.

Then she turned and went upstairs, her shoes clicking softly with each step.

The Sunday Paper

Alex and Alberta Jefferson were on their way down to the street, dressed in their Sunday best and bound for First Baptist Church just a few blocks away. Alex whistled softly as he walked, his Bible tucked under one arm and his hat tilted just a bit off-center. Alberta followed a step behind, stiff and composed, a clutch bag in her gloved hands and a narrow-brimmed hat pinned precisely over her curls.

They were halfway down the stairs when a door opened below. Dr. Roddie stepped out into the hallway, dressed in a pressed gray suit with a deep blue tie, his shoes shined to a high polish. He moved quickly, adjusting the cuffs of his jacket as he closed the door behind him with practiced ease.

Alex brightened. "Mornin', Doc!" he called cheerfully. "A man dressed like that on a Sunday's gotta be headed to the Lord's house."

Roddie looked up with a warm smile. "Good morning, Mr. Jefferson. Mrs. Jefferson." He nodded to them both. "I've got to meet with a patient. Urgent matter."

Alberta's posture stiffened. Her gloved hand tightened slightly on the stair rail. "On a Sunday?" she asked, coolly. "Must be serious."

"It is," Roddie said, his tone even. "Her husband passed suddenly last night. She's… not in her right mind. Needs someone to help her hold steady."

Alex's face fell. "That's awful," he muttered. "Poor woman."

Roddie nodded, his smile fading just enough to signal respect.

"Have a good day," Roddie said simply.

Then he gave a polite nod and stepped past them with quiet urgency. His cologne lingered for a moment—sharp, clean, layered with something faintly herbal—as he disappeared around the corner and out the front door.

Alberta didn't move right away. Her eyes remained on the spot where he'd stood.

Alex gave her a nudge with his elbow. "What's got you lookin' like that?"

She blinked. "Nothing."

The sanctuary was hot with the kind of still heat that settled in your clothes and made your skin feel like damp cotton. Alberta Jefferson sat in the third pew from the front, an old Bible resting in her lap—the one that had belonged to her mother. In one hand, she worked a fan slow and steady, its faded cardboard edge fluttering through the heavy air.

Beside her, Alex was slumped slightly, breathing through his mouth, eyes closed. His hands rested on his knees, slack. A soft snore escaped his lips, just loud enough to be noticed but not loud enough to scold.

Alberta elbowed him lightly. He stirred but didn't wake. She sighed and turned her attention back to the pulpit.

Reverend Bill Thompson was in full swing, his voice rising and falling like a tide against the wooden walls of the sanctuary.

"I tell you now," the reverend said, wiping sweat from his brow with a handkerchief, "the Devil don't always come dressed in red and breathing fire. Sometimes he wears a pressed white shirt and tells you he can fix what only the Lord can mend."

Scattered murmurs of "Amen" rippled through the pews.

He held up his Bible, pages worn thin at the corners.

"Leviticus nineteen, thirty-one," he said, voice rising. "*'Regard not them that have familiar spirits, neither seek after wizards, to be defiled by them: I am the Lord your God!'*"

The words echoed off the wood-paneled walls like a warning bell.

"Some of you sitting here might've already opened your door to him. Might've lit his candles. Might've let him whisper in your ear, put his hands where only prayer belongs."

"I tell you now," Reverend Thompson said, dabbing his brow with a handkerchief, "the Word says in Psalm 118, verse 8: *'It is better to trust in the Lord than to put confidence in man.'* That's not just a suggestion—it's a warning."

Soft murmurs of agreement stirred in the pews.

"Man will fail you," he continued. "He'll promise you peace and give you confusion. He'll tell you he's got the answer—some secret, some special knowledge—but if it don't come from God, it won't last. It won't heal."

Alberta nodded along, tight-lipped. She didn't look at anyone. But her mind had already slipped elsewhere—back to the hallway, back to that quiet moment when Roddie smiled without speaking. That apartment with its smells of smoke and oil and shadowed promises. The way he watched people. The way he *knew* things.

The reverend's voice thundered now, nearly shaking the dust from the rafters.

"Don't go putting your hope in men with smooth words and strange ways. Don't go searching for light in places the Lord never lit!"

"Amen," Alberta whispered, her voice nearly lost beneath the swell of others.

Beside her, Alex snorted and sat up abruptly, rubbing his face. "Did I miss the benediction?"

♦♦♦♦♦♦

That afternoon, the apartment was quiet when they returned, save for the distant hum of a neighbor's radio. Alberta moved through the kitchen with practiced rhythm. A pan sizzled. The kettle clicked once, then whistled. The bread was toasted just the way Alex liked it—golden and crisp but not brittle.

At the small kitchen table, Alex rustled the newspaper open with the enthusiasm of a man who rarely read past the headlines.

Alberta set a plate down in front of him: ham and cheese, a few pickles, a dollop of mustard on the side. She moved to retrieve the tea from the stove when his voice cut through the room.

"Mmm! Smells good," he said.

She smiled as she stirred sugar into the tea.

He turned a page and let out a soft whistle.

"Well now," he muttered. "Ain't that something..."

Alberta raised an eyebrow, still turned away.

"What?"

He held the paper up, folding it with one hand so he could read and eat at the same time. "Local man dead in fire. Office blaze late last night. Happened over on Gay Street."

Alberta walked back over and set the tea beside him. He barely looked up.

She glanced down at the page. The headline stretched across the top of the local section:

LOCAL MAN DEAD IN FIRE

Real estate agent Douglas Gable was found deceased in his downtown office after a blaze broke out in the early morning hours…

Her eyes scanned quickly.

Survived by his wife, Edna Gable.

Alberta's hand flew to her mouth.

She stared at the name, the paragraph, the picture of the building, blackened and broken.

Alex crunched a pickle and took another bite of his sandwich.

Alberta didn't speak. She didn't sit. She stood still as the kitchen clock ticking above the doorway. Her eyes were wide, her breath short. She remembered Edna's face. The neat skirt suit. The lingering scent of lavender and lemon oil.

She knew where Roddie had run off to earlier in the day.

"Sweetheart?" Alex called from the table. "Mind getting me some more tea?"

But Alberta was no longer in the kitchen.

She wasn't in the hallway either.

The apartment was still.

Alex looked up, puzzled. "Bertie?"

Nothing.

The kettle on the stove had stopped whistling. The room was silent except for the soft voice of Alberta praying in her bedroom.

Rusty Nails

The night before the fire…

The roast was done by five.
Edna had peeled the potatoes by noon, let them sit in cold water while she swept the floor and pressed the napkins. Now they were boiled, mashed smooth with butter and a pinch of salt, just the way Douglas liked them—at least the way he used to.

She laid two plates on the kitchen table, setting them across from each other. Napkins folded neat. Fork on the left. Knife and spoon on the right. She lit the small lamp on the counter, its yellow glow softening the edges of the room.

The radio buzzed from the parlor—something slow and brassy drifting out of WNOX—but she barely heard it. She glanced at the clock. Ten after five. Then the door. Edna stepped to the front of the house, unlatched the screen door and leaned out. The street was quiet, golden with sunset. A boy down the block tossed a ball against a fence. A few sparrows chattered in the hedges. No Douglas. No car in the driveway.

She waited a moment longer, then turned back inside.

In the kitchen, she took the roast from the oven, its scent filling the room like a promise half-kept. She carved a few slices and spooned potatoes onto a plate. Just one. She left his empty.

The radio crackled as the song ended, and a cheerful announcer launched into a weather report. Edna crossed the room and turned the dial until the voice gave way to static, then silence.

She sat. And sat.

The fork clinked lightly against the plate, though she barely lifted it to her mouth. Her eyes drifted toward the door, then the clock, then nowhere at all. Her fingers curled slightly in her lap, gripping nothing.

She didn't cry. Not yet. But the tears were close, lining her lashes like glass waiting to break.

She reached for the plate again, tried one more bite, and set it down. Cold now.

The house was still. Her chest ached with the weight of unsaid things. She breathed deep, slow, and stood.

Tomorrow, she would ask him again—where he went. Why he stayed away. If he remembered her voice.

The morning of the fire...

The sound of a straight razor gliding over stubble filled the tiled bathroom. Douglas Gable leaned toward the mirror, careful and mechanical in his motions. He nicked himself just under the chin—nothing deep, but enough to leave a bright bead of red behind. He hissed through his teeth and reached for a square of toilet paper to blot it. A smudge of blood remained on the porcelain sink.

"Douglas?" Edna called gently from the hallway. "Are you hungry?"

No reply.

She poked her head around the door, a towel in her hands. "Eggs and biscuits are still warm."

Douglas didn't answer. He buttoned his collar and grabbed his coat from the hook.

She followed him into the hall. "You working today?"

"Yeah."

"On a *Saturday*?" she asked, her tone soft but puzzled.

He groaned. "Big deadline. We're behind."

"You didn't say anything about a deadline last week."

"I'm saying it now."

She watched him move toward the front door. "What time you think you'll be home?"

He sighed, hand on the knob. "I don't know, Edna. Late."

"Should I still cook?"

He turned just enough to roll his eyes. "I *have to go.*"

The door shut behind him with a hard finality.

Edna stood alone in the quiet parlor. She sank slowly onto the couch, still holding the towel, her face blank. A single tear trailed down her cheek. Then another.

After a moment, she stood.

She walked to the bedroom closet and pulled down one of his ties—navy with thin red stripes. As she held it, a familiar but *foreign* scent caught her attention. She brought it to her nose.

Lavender.

Not hers.

Her eyes flared. Her breath quickened.

She stared at her reflection in the hallway mirror, searching her own face for a reaction. Then she balled the tie in her fist and tossed it into the bathroom waste bin.

Outside, the backyard waited in a hush. Edna crossed it barefoot, heading for the tool shed. Inside, she found a storage nook with broken flowerpots, rusted tools, and an old cigar box tucked behind a shelf.

Inside the box: four long, crooked nails. Orange with rust.

She found a hammer on the workbench.

Stomping back inside, her bare heels loud against the worn floorboards, she made straight for the bathroom. The mirror caught her face—red-eyed, jaw tight, breathing like a piston—but she didn't stop.

She crouched low over the sink, the faint smear of Douglas's blood still gleaming on the porcelain.

"Lyin' son of a bitch," she muttered, her voice rough and trembling.

She grabbed the first nail and dragged its head through the blood, twisting it slowly as though making a point.

"You think I'm some kind of fool."

One by one, she rubbed each nail in the blood, whispering to herself between clenched teeth—words half-prayer, half-curse.

When she was done, all four nail heads shimmered dully with rust and red in the morning light. And Edna Gable—barefoot, shaking, heart broken clean through—stood up straight and carried them outside.

Then she stepped out into the yard and began driving the nails into the earth—one at each corner of the house.

A neighbor folding sheets on a nearby clothesline looked over.

"Morning, Edna," she called, puzzled.

Edna didn't answer. She was crying now, the kind of cry that came from somewhere deep and burning. But her hands didn't shake. Her aim was true.

The hammer fell.

Again. And again. And again.

"It's a Fine Coffin"

It was a little before noon when Delphine Tucker arrived back at the apartment on North Central. Her hand held tight to her purse strap, her steps steady but unsure.

As she approached the stoop, another woman arrived—tall, slender, and well-dressed in a modest yellow blouse and pressed skirt. A little girl walked beside her, no more than seven, with braids tied in bright ribbons and a pair of patent leather shoes that clicked on the pavement.

Delphine smiled. "Well, don't you look pretty," she said to the child. "That's a lovely dress you've got on."

The girl beamed. "Thank you, ma'am!"

Her mother gave a small smile. "She's excited—it's her first piano lesson."

"Is that so?" Delphine said. "I used to play a little, back when I was a girl. You stick with it now, you hear?"

The girl nodded, proud and eager, and together they stepped inside. At the landing, they parted ways—mother and daughter continuing up to the Jeffersons', while Delphine turned toward Dr. Roddie's door and knocked twice, just as before.

He answered in a crisp shirt and suspenders, the light behind him warm and dim.

"Mrs. Tucker," he said. "Come on in."

She stepped inside, settling into the now-familiar chair near the altar. The small table still held its clutter of jars, feathers, and folded paper. The faint aroma of herbs and burnt wax hung in the air.

"Would you like some water?" he asked, already reaching.

She shook her head. "No thank you. I'm fine."

He sat across from her, folding his hands. "How can I help you today? Any developments with your sister?"

Delphine grimaced, her gloved fingers curling. "Not really. She did what you said. Put the mix under her pillow, wore the oil. At first, Willis was… different. Sweeter. More affectionate. But then, yesterday, she brought up marriage again and he laughed in her face."

Roddie leaned back with a sigh, shaking his head. "Oh my… that's unfortunate. But don't get discouraged. There's still hope. Sometimes the spirit of a man has to be… guided."

He paused and grabbed his notebook.

Faintly, the annoying clinking notes of a piano trickled down from above. The tune was childish, halting. Roddie's jaw tensed, but he said nothing. He turned back to Delphine, face composed as he flipped through to a certain page.

"Here's what she needs to do," Roddie said pointing to a page titled **LOVE**. "She must ask Willis to supper. They need to share a meal, just the two of them. But before she meets him, she needs to rub her arms and legs with a mixture of coffee grounds and vinegar."

Delphine recoiled slightly. "Won't he smell it?"

Roddie's gaze narrowed, his tone clipped. "Ma'am, do you want your sister to have a husband?"

She hesitated, then nodded.

"Then please, do as I say."

He rose and moved to a shelf, selecting a few things from a small wooden box. The piano overhead tinkled a sour note. He stopped mid-motion, his hand tightening around the box's lid. Then, shaking it off, he resumed his work.

"Now—there's more," he said, returning. "Your sister will need one of his shoes. Just one. She must take a sewing needle and put it in her mouth. Don't prick herself, but it must be wet with her spit. Then she sticks that needle into the rubber part of the sole—sideways. Where it won't touch his foot when he walks."

Delphine's eyebrows rose, but she said nothing.

Roddie reached for a small necklace—twine with a charm, no larger than a dime.

"This is a gris-gris. Your sister must wear it. She cannot take it off, not even to bathe."

He handed it to her, his face solemn.

"I'm confident this will work," he said.

Delphine opened her purse.

"Thank you," she whispered. "How much is your fee for this?"

"Eighty for the session," he said, "and twenty more for the gris-gris."

She nodded and gave him the full amount.

As she left, he closed the door gently behind her.

A few moments later, Roddie stormed into the kitchen. Lizzie sat at the table, glasses perched on her nose, reading the newspaper with a glass of tea in hand.

Without a word, he grabbed the broom from the corner.

"Obie…" she started.

He raised the broom and jabbed the ceiling hard—once, twice, three times. The muffled piano faltered above.

"Damn piano," he muttered.

Lizzie sipped her tea, unbothered. "You can barely hear it in here."

"I've got to get cleaned up for the funeral," he said suddenly, placing the broom back. He moved swiftly to the bedroom and within a minute he was standing in the doorway.

"I'll be back in a while."

He was out the door before she could ask if he wanted her to go with him.

♦♦♦♦♦♦

The piano echoed faintly through the floorboards above, soft and steady—Alex was still finishing his Saturday lesson, and Alberta had slipped out quietly, hat in hand. The morning air had cooled, just slightly, as she walked the short distance to the small brick church nestled between two sycamores. The funeral sign out front was handwritten and pinned to a wooden easel: *In Loving Memory of Douglas C. Gable.*

Inside, the sanctuary was hushed, heavy with the weight of grief and floral arrangements. A simple closed coffin stood near the pulpit, flanked by vases of lilies and two brass candle stands. Edna Gable stood nearby, receiving condolences with a stiff grace, her black dress neat and her gloved hands folded in front of her after each handshake.

Alberta stepped into the line and joined the slow procession of mourners. She kept her eyes forward, polite but distant, until the doors opened again behind her. Dr. Obie Lee Roddie entered the chapel, hat in hand, dressed in a clean gray suit with a navy pocket square. His shoes shined like polished glass. Alberta's eyes flicked toward him. He offered a smile. She did not return it.

He fell into line behind her.

When Alberta reached the front, Edna recognized her with a faint spark of familiarity. "Alberta," she said, softly, pulling her into a gentle embrace.

"I'm sorry for your loss," Alberta murmured. "We have to get together sometime soon. Maybe lunch."

Edna gave a small nod, her eyes tired. "I'd like that."

Alberta stepped away, moving to a pew near the middle aisle. She sat, adjusting her gloves, but her eyes never left the side of the church.

Roddie was still in line. When he reached Edna, her whole demeanor shifted. Her stiff composure seemed to crack just a little. She pulled him close, her hand gripping his arm in a way that caught a few nearby glances.

"Dr. Roddie," she whispered, her voice a low, urgent tremor, "please... please don't judge me."

He pulled away just enough to look her in the eyes, offering a faint half-smile and a slow shake of his head. "Thank you for coming," she murmured, his voice too low for anyone else to hear. "Maybe we can talk about this after the service. Come find me in the cemetery."

Then he leaned in close again, his lips near her ear, and whispered something more. From her pew, Alberta couldn't hear the words, but she saw their effect. Edna's eyes, already red-rimmed, widened in surprise, and a fresh wave of sadness seemed to wash over her. She shook her head slightly, a small, involuntary gesture of disbelief.

Roddie gave a final, serious nod and stepped away. To Alberta's quiet dismay, he slid into the same pew as her.

"It's a fine coffin," he said softly. "Beautiful flowers."

Alberta turned her face away, watching the front of the church as a new figure approached Edna—an elderly woman in a long black veil who trembled as she embraced her. Douglas' mother.

The old woman was inconsolable. Her wails filled the church like a rising tide.

Reverend Bill Thompson stepped in gently and helped guide both women to their seats near the front.

He cleared his throat, adjusted his Bible, and began the service.

"We come together today not just in mourning, but in remembrance. Douglas Gable was a man of deep faith, a devoted husband, and a loyal son. He was taken from us too soon, but we rest in the promise of the Lord..."

As he spoke, Edna remained composed, her face like stone—save for the slightest, unmistakable roll of her eyes when the preacher called Douglas "devoted." Alberta caught it and blinked.

Beside Edna, the old woman rocked gently in her seat, clutching a folded handkerchief to her lips.

The preacher paused once, mid-sermon, to kneel beside her. He placed a steadying hand on her knee. When her sobs quieted, he returned to the pulpit.

He closed with a prayer and a kind invitation.

"There will be a short graveside service at Old Gray Cemetery, just around the corner. All who wish to attend are welcome."

As the organ began to play, Alberta's fingers tightened slightly around her purse strap. She could feel Roddie beside her, calm and still. Too still.

And she knew—without knowing how she knew—that whatever he had whispered into his ear, it wasn't grief—it was a pact.

♦♦♦♦♦♦

The walk up the hill was quiet except for the soft rustle of leaves and the faint creak of leather shoes on gravel. Alberta Jefferson moved with care between old tombstones, their weathered faces half-sunk into the grass like tired watchers of the dead. The sun was dipping behind the trees now, casting long shadows across Old Gray Cemetery.

Ahead, a small cluster of mourners stood in a crescent near an open grave. Edna Gable stood steady at the center, surrounded by family and friends. Alberta made her way closer, keeping her eyes forward. A long white hearse was parked nearby, its chrome grille catching the last glimmers of sunlight. A group of solemn men gathered at the back, preparing to do what gravity and grief required.

Alberta paused near a crooked grave marker, just in time to see Dr. Roddie approaching from the opposite end of the cemetery. He moved at an unhurried pace. His hands slipped casually into his coat pockets before he paused beside a broken headstone. Without fanfare, he bent slightly and plucked a few sprigs of grass, then stooped to collect two small stones, which he tucked away into the lining of his coat. Alberta frowned. She didn't know what he was doing, but she didn't like it.

The preacher's voice broke across the hush: solemn, steady, familiar. Alberta stepped forward just as the final prayer began. Douglas' mother sobbed openly, trembling in her black veil. Edna leaned down and wrapped her arms around the older woman, pressing her cheek gently against her shoulder.

At the grave's edge, two men worked the straps slowly, carefully lowering Douglas Gable into the earth. The casket rocked gently as it settled, the finality of the moment hitting like the thud of clods on wood. When the first shovelful of dirt landed, it made Edna flinch. Still, she stayed upright, her hand clutching her mother-in-law's tightly.

One by one, the mourners began to drift away, offering nods and brief condolences before stepping off the burial hill. Alberta approached her old friend. She opened her arms and embraced Edna with a firm, measured grip.

"I'll see you soon," Alberta said softly.

Edna's face, unreadable a moment before, softened. "I hope so."

As Alberta turned to leave, she heard footsteps behind her. She slowed but didn't stop. Roddie passed close by Edna, offering no words—only a faint, reassuring smile and a gentle squeeze on her forearm. Edna met his eyes and nodded once, and that was enough.

From the hill's edge, Alberta watched it all. She watched him walk away, hands back in his coat pockets, as though he was enjoying a Sunday stroll through the park.

♦♦♦♦♦♦

The apartment was quiet, steeped in the hush that only deep night could bring. A single candle flickered near the kitchen sink, casting long, crooked shadows across the linoleum.

From the hallway, Lizzie stood barefoot, her hand curled gently around the edge of the beaded curtain. She peered into the conjure room, her face lit faintly by the low orange glow within.

Roddie was already at work.

He hadn't noticed her—didn't turn, didn't speak. He stood in his shirtsleeves, coat folded over a chair, carefully placing objects on the altar like pieces in a story only he knew how to tell. A handful of stones. Grass from the cemetery. A red cloth unrolled with slow reverence.

Lizzie's brow pinched softly, but she said nothing. Her eyes lingered for just a moment longer. Then she pulled back quietly, the beads barely clinking as she turned and disappeared down the hall.

Inside, the air was dense with smoke and memory.

Roddie muttered something low under his breath—words old and heavy, passed down like scars. He lit a candle with a match and burned a small strip of paper in a dish, watching as the fire curled it inward until only ash remained.

He placed the stones one by one around the dish in a circle, whispering something with each placement.

Then, faint and unwelcome, came the sound of music.

Piano. Just a few notes at first, aimless and soft.

Then the start of a melody—something upbeat, careless.

Roddie's eyes shifted to the ceiling. His jaw clenched.

He didn't speak right away, just stood still, the muscles in his neck tightening.

Then a quiet grumble under his breath: "Of all the nights…"

The piano continued, like a child showing off. He exhaled slowly and returned his focus to the altar.

He closed his eyes and pressed both hands flat on the table. The room dimmed further in the candlelight, shadows leaning in.

The piano played on.

But Roddie had already slipped somewhere deeper—where the music couldn't follow.

♦♦♦♦♦♦

The next morning, the sun filtered softly through the lace curtains, casting a checkered glow across the Jefferson's breakfast table. Alex sat with one elbow resting on the edge, a steaming mug of coffee in hand and the *Knoxville News-Sentinel* spread wide before him. He glanced over headlines about the weather, a steel shortage, and a city council dispute on trolley fares.

Alberta moved about the kitchen with quiet purpose. She refilled her husband's cup without a word, setting the pot gently back on the stove.

"Thanks, darling," Alex said, barely looking up.

She pulled out a chair and sat beside him. Her posture was composed, but there was a tension in her shoulders that didn't go unnoticed—at least not by someone paying attention.

"Alex," she said slowly, folding her hands in her lap. "Do you remember Edna Gable?"

He didn't lower the paper. "Don't think so."

"She was Edna Monroe before she got married. Her uncle used to live across the street from me when I was in high school."

Alex blinked behind his glasses and furrowed his brow. "Maybe. That name sounds familiar."

Alberta leaned in just slightly. "I saw her last week. She was coming out of Dr. Roddie's apartment."

That got his attention. He lowered the paper, finally looking at her fully. "The voodoo man downstairs?" She gave a stiff nod. "Yes."

"What for?"

"She said she was having trouble with her husband."

Alex tilted his head. "That's unfortunate."

Alberta sat up straighter, her voice firmer now.

"Two days later, he was dead."

Alex froze mid-sip. "What?"

"That fire downtown," she added. "The one in the office building. He was working late that night."

Alex set his mug down slowly, the clink on the saucer sharp and telling. "Lord, I read about that. Tragic. But you're saying... you think Mr. Roddie had something to do with it?"

"I don't know," Alberta said, eyes narrowing. "I just know it doesn't sit right. That poor woman was at her wits' end. And now her husband's gone."

Alex ran a hand through his hair. "I know that boy's a little kooky, always burnin' herbs and chanting, but I didn't think he'd... you know. Do harm."

Alberta's lips pressed into a tight line. "I'm not

accusing nobody. But something's wrong. I feel it in my bones."

Alex looked down at the newspaper, then back up at his wife. For once, he didn't have a joke or a shrug to offer.

And Alberta just stared at the window, where the sun was still shining like nothing had changed.

♦♦♦♦♦♦

A mile away, the midday sun warmed the wooden slats of a park bench. From across the street, the grand entrance of the Andrew Johnson Hotel gleamed. Dr. Obie Lee Roddie sat, calmly smoking a cigarette, looking for all the world like a young man simply enjoying his lunch break. But his eyes, always watching, were fixed on the hotel doors.

A few minutes later, a woman in a crisp waitress uniform hurried across the street, clutching her purse. She sat at the far end of the bench, not looking at him directly.

"Dr. Roddie," she said, her voice low.

"Beatrice," he replied with a nod. "You have something for me?"

"I think so," she said, her own eyes darting around the park. "There's a man. Comes in for lunch every day around noon. From the Brookside Mills, I think. Wears the same sad expression every time. Stanley, is his name, I think..."

Roddie remained silent, letting her talk.

"Well, today he was talking to another mill worker who came in with him," Beatrice continued. "Grumbling. Said some young man is about to get the promotion he'd been after for years. Said he felt like he was cursed with really bad luck."

Roddie allowed a small, knowing smile to touch his lips. "And does he have any other troubles?"

"He gets awful headaches," she said. "Always rubbing his temples."

"I see," Roddie said. He reached into his coat pocket, and in a single, smooth motion, placed a few neatly folded dollar bills on the bench between them. "For your trouble."

Beatrice discreetly swept the money into her hand and tucked it into her apron. "What should I tell him?"

"The next time he comes in," Roddie said, his voice soft but clear, "when you pour his coffee, you tell him you heard of a man. A doctor over at the Riverside Apartments on North Central who helps folks with... burdens. I'm in 203. You tell him I can help with his headaches. And his luck."

"Yes, Doctor," she said. She stood up, smoothing her uniform. "I have to get back."

She hurried back across the street and disappeared into the hotel. Roddie remained on the bench for a moment longer, his gaze fixed on the grand entrance. The seed was planted. Now, he just had to wait for the roots to take hold.

More Music

The following day, the air in the conjure room was already thick with the scent of burnt herbs and something sharp, like vinegar. Dr. Roddie moved with a quiet, deliberate purpose. He took a clean slip of paper and, with a frantic, focused energy, scribbled something on it—words or symbols, it was impossible to tell. He placed the paper on a small tin plate in the center of the table. From a dark wooden cabinet, he retrieved a vial of amber-colored oil, uncorked it, and poured the entire contents over the paper, watching it turn translucent. He struck a match, the hiss and flare loud in the quiet room, and touched it to the saturated paper. It erupted in a smokeless blue flame, curling inward until only a greasy black ash remained.

Knock. Knock.

Roddie answered the door to find a man fidgeting on the landing, his hat held tight in both hands. He was around forty-five, with tired lines around his eyes and the stoop of a man who had spent too many years looking down.

"I'm… I'm looking for a Dr. Roddie?" the man asked, his voice timid, uncertain he was in the right place.

Roddie's face broke into a warm, disarming smile. "Yes. I'm Obie Roddie. How may I help you?"

The man swallowed, his grip tightening on his hat. "My name is Stanley Carr, sir. A lady... she works over at the Andrew Johnson Hotel... she said you were a man who could help folks."

"I hope I can," Roddie said, his voice smooth and

reassuring. "I will certainly do all I can. Please, come in. Right this way."

He ushered the man into the hallway, through the beaded curtain and into the conjure room. They sat across from each other at the small table, the plate of fresh ash between them.

"Now," Roddie began gently. "How can I help you?"

Stanley Carr shifted uncomfortably in the worn red chair. "Well," he started, his gaze fixed on his twisting hat brim. "I've been working at the mill for sixteen years. Over in packing. I've only missed one day of work in all that time, and that was when my momma died. I'm a good employee. I'm always on time, always stay late when they ask. I only make fifty-five cents an hour. They're bringing in new hires at fifty cents."

He paused, swallowing hard. "I've been passed over for a promotion three, maybe four times. Just today, some young fellow who's chummy with the plant manager got promoted to supervisor. He ain't been there a full year. Took credit for an idea I had, and now he's getting a bump in pay and better hours." He finally looked up, his eyes pleading. "I'm just so stressed out, Doctor. I feel like I can't get ahead." He rubbed his temple with two fingers. "Sorry. All this has given me horrible headaches."

Roddie leaned back, observing him, his face a mask of empathy. Then, Stanley's last words seemed to click into place. An idea surfaced.

"Please excuse me, sir," Roddie said, standing abruptly. "One moment."

He slipped out of the room and walked into the kitchen where Lizzie sat at the table, her glasses perched on her nose, reading a book. He leaned down and kissed her on the cheek. She looked up, puzzled by the interruption. Without a word, he went to a large bin in the corner and reached inside.

"Obie?" Lizzie asked as he pulled out a handful of dusty brown potatoes.

She smirked, a knowing look in her eyes. Then she heard it, too. A clunky, hesitant clatter from above. The piano.

Roddie froze. His face, calm and professional a moment before, tightened into a grimace. One of the potatoes slipped from his grasp and thudded onto the linoleum floor. He shook his head. Lizzie sighed, bent down to pick up the potato, and placed it firmly back in his hand.

"Now, Obie…" she said, her voice a soft warning. He took a deep, steadying breath, his composure returning like a shroud. When he re-entered the conjure room, he was holding the handful of potatoes. Stanley stared, puzzled.

Roddie extended his hands. "Now, Mr. Carr, for your headaches. At night, while you are sleeping, I want you to place these in your shoes. Two or three in each shoe. Then you place the shoes under your bed."

As he spoke, he could still hear the music from upstairs. He fought to keep the aggravation from his face. Stanley, looking bewildered but desperate enough to trust, took the potatoes and put them in his large coat pockets.

Roddie then flipped through his black notebook until he came to a page titled **RETRIBUTION**. He scanned the scribbled words and then handed Stanley a fresh piece of paper and a pencil. "Here. Write the name of the man who has stolen your idea."

Stanley dutifully wrote the name. Roddie took the paper and placed it on a clean plate. He reached under the table and retrieved a heavy brick, setting it firmly on top of the paper. He moved to the cabinet, got a vial of oil, and poured it liberally over the brick, letting it soak down into the paper beneath. Stanley watched, his mouth slightly agape. Roddie then took a small vial filled with clear oil and set it on the table. From a jar, he pulled a sprig of rosemary, plucked a few leaves, and dropped them into the vial.

"Now," he said, his voice once again low and confident. "Tomorrow, before you go to work, I want you to rub this on your body. On your chest. While you are looking into a mirror, as you rub it into your skin, I want you to say, loudly and confidently, that you are worthy of a better job. Don't just say it. *Mean it.*"

The piano upstairs hit a series of sour, clunky notes. Roddie caught himself scowling and smoothed his expression.

"Then," he continued, "you go speak to the plant manager. You tell him you have been loyal, and you want more responsibilities. Do you understand?"

"Yes, Doctor," Stanley said, his eyes wide with a mixture of awe and hope.

"You must believe it when you say it."

Stanley nodded.

The music got louder, a clumsy, enthusiastic march. Roddie's jaw tightened. He stopped himself, forcing a polite closure. "Thank you for coming by, Mr. Carr."

An awkward silence hung in the air.

"My fee," Roddie said, his voice flat, "is forty-five

dollars."

Stanley's eyes widened in dismay. "Doctor, I... I'm afraid I don't have that much. I work at the mill."

A flicker of aggravation crossed Roddie's face before being replaced by professional courtesy. He was tired. The piano was grating on his last nerve.

"How about twenty-five dollars, sir?" he asked, his tone polite but firm. "Can you afford that?"

Stanley nodded, pulling his worn wallet from his back pocket. "Yes, sir."

"When you get your promotion," Roddie added, "you can return with the additional twenty."

"Yes, sir! I'll be happy to," Stanley said, his voice filled with renewed conviction. He counted out the money and then extended a hand. Roddie shook it firmly.

Stanley exited, clutching the vial of rosemary oil like a precious jewel, his shoulders already seeming a little straighter than when he had arrived.

The front door clicked shut, and Stanley's heavy footsteps faded down the stairwell. Dr. Roddie didn't pause. He turned from the door and moved directly back through the beaded curtain into the conjure room. The air still smelled of burnt paper and Stanley's quiet desperation.

He went to a low shelf, past the jars of roots and feathers, and selected a heavy ceramic crock, dark and unadorned. He uncorked it, the stopper making a soft *pop* in the still room.

Lizzie stuck her head through the beaded curtain, her glasses still perched on her nose. "Honey, what do you want for supper?"

Roddie didn't answer immediately. He tipped the crock and poured a fine, gray powder into the palm of his left hand. The ashes were cool and silky against his skin. From the doorway, Lizzie's eyebrow arched in silent curiosity.

Not missing a beat, Roddie looked up, his expression shifting instantly from intense focus to pleasant domesticity. "It doesn't matter, dear," he said, his voice smooth. "What would you like?"

She considered for a moment. "Uh, well, I was thinking about that ham we have in the refrigerator. I might make some carrots. Maybe some potatoes if you didn't give them all away."

A low, soft snicker escaped Roddie's lips. It was a sound of private amusement, gone almost as soon as it appeared.

Lizzie couldn't help but ask, her tone gentle but direct. "Obie, what are you doing?"

He smiled then—a closed, private smile that didn't quite reach his eyes. "Just something I need to take care of, dear."

With that, he cupped his hand carefully around the ashes and turned, brushing past her toward the front door. He was halfway into the hall when he turned back, his face suddenly bright and cheerful again.

"Oh, and ham and potatoes sounds wonderful! A great idea!"

Roddie slipped into the hallway, pulling the door shut behind him with a soft click. The air was still and smelled of dust and old wood. He paused, his head cocked, listening. He peered down the narrow hall toward the front of the building, then craned his neck to look up the stairwell. No one. The building was quiet, caught in the late afternoon lull.

He didn't waste a moment. He sprinted up the

stairs, his movements surprisingly swift and silent, his hard-soled shoes barely making a sound on the worn wooden treads. He stopped just outside the Jeffersons' door, his heart beating a steady, focused rhythm.

With the careful precision of a surgeon, he opened his cupped palm and began to pour the ashes, letting them fall in a thin, unbroken gray line directly in front of their welcome mat. The powder settled softly on the floorboards, a stark, deliberate barrier. After the last of the ash dropped from his hand, he rubbed his palms together, wiping them clean of the residue.

"There," he whispered to the empty hallway, a small, satisfied smile touching his lips.

He wasted no time, turning and rushing back down the stairs with the same urgent quiet. He slipped back inside his own apartment, the scent of frying ham and Lizzie's presence instantly grounding him. He went straight to the sink and turned the faucet, vigorously washing his hands as his wife moved between the stove and the counter, preparing supper.

He dried his hands on a dish towel, came up behind her, and gave her a kiss on the cheek.

"I'm getting hungry," he said, his voice light and cheerful.

Lizzie gave him a strange look, a trace of puzzlement in her otherwise calm eyes. She didn't know precisely what he had been up to, but she knew the look of a man who had just settled a score.

♦♦♦♦♦♦

Later that night, on the other side of town, the scent of chicken and dumplings simmered on the stove, a thick, comforting aroma that filled Glenda's small kitchen. It was the smell of home, of warmth, of a life she was trying to build, but tonight, it was fighting a losing battle against the sharp, sour tang of vinegar.

"I feel like a fool, Della," Glenda said, wrinkling her nose at the brown, gritty paste in the bowl before her. "The powder he gave me just made me sneeze all night, and that oil smelled like old lemons. Now this? He's going to think I've been pickling my own feet."

"It's not for him to smell, it's for him to feel," Delphine insisted, her voice low and urgent. She held up the small twine necklace Dr. Roddie had given her, the charm no larger than a dime . "And you have to wear this. He said don't you dare take it off, not even to bathe."

Glenda sighed and leaned forward, allowing her sister to fasten the gris-gris around her neck. It felt cool against her skin. "And what happens if he still says no?"

"He won't," Delphine said, with more conviction than she felt. "Now, do it. Before he gets here."

Begrudgingly, Glenda dipped her fingers into the bowl of used coffee grounds and vinegar and began to rub the coarse mixture onto her arms and legs, her face twisted in disgust. "Della, he's going to smell this. He ain't going to want to come near me!"

"You have to!" Delphine pleaded. "Just trust Dr. Roddie."

"And how in the world am I supposed to get a needle in his shoe?" Glenda asked, gesturing with a gritty hand. "Should I ask him to hold still while I do it?"

"I have an idea," Delphine said, her eyes alight

with sudden inspiration. "When he comes in, you tell him he looks tired. You get him to take his shoes off and sit on the couch. You give him a foot rub, and I'll sit with you both, keep him talking about his day. Then, you tell him dinner's ready. When you two go into the kitchen, I'll stay behind. I'll say I need to use the washroom before I head home. That's when I'll do it."

Glenda stared at her sister, a mixture of horror and admiration on her face. She shook her head slowly but finally nodded. "Alright, Della. Alright."

She finished applying the strange poultice and went to check on the dumplings, her nose wrinkled with every step. As she disappeared into the kitchen's steam, Delphine pulled a small sewing kit from her purse. Just then, a knock sounded at the door.

Willis Greene stuck his head in. "Anybody home?" Delphine's face broke into a wide smile. "Willis! Come on in, honey. Glenda's just getting supper ready." She gave him a warm hug as he stepped inside.

Glenda emerged from the kitchen, wiping her hands on her apron, a big smile on her face.

Willis sniffed the air as he entered, a slight frown on his face. "What's that smell?" he asked.

Glenda froze. Her heart hammered against her ribs. *He can smell it,* she thought, the sour scent of vinegar and coffee grounds suddenly feeling like a suffocating cloud around her.

His frown then dissolved into a wide, appreciative grin. "Oh! That smells like chicken and dumplings."

Glenda let out a breath and a relieved smile bloomed on her face. "It is. Almost ready."

His eyes remained on her, and he pointed toward her neck. "That looks new."

Her hand flew instinctively to the twine necklace, the small charm cool against her skin. "Oh, this?" she said, her voice a little shaky. "Just a little something Della gave me."

He nodded, his interest already passing. Glenda's heart was still fluttering, but she managed to look him over. "You look tired. Long day?"

Willis smirked, preening just a little. "Not really. My boss, Mr. Henderson, he took me out for a big lunch today. We sat around and talked for a couple of hours."

Glenda's smile tightened. "That's exciting. Come over here and sit down. Let me rub your feet."

Willis shrugged, a pleased look on his face. "Well, if you insist." He kicked off his shoes by the door and settled onto the couch. As Glenda knelt and began to rub his feet, Delphine sat in the armchair opposite them.

"So how is work going, Willis?" Delphine asked, her voice bright.

Willis beamed. "It's going great! That's what Mr. Henderson and I were talking about. A new role for me opened up at the mill yesterday. Supervisor for the day shift. The hours might be longer, but it's got a big increase in pay."

"Oh, Willis, that's wonderful!" Glenda said, and this time her smile was genuine. She rubbed his feet for a little while longer, the rhythm steady and soothing. "Are you hungry? I made chicken and dumplins. Got some green beans, too."

"Am I ever!" he said, hopping up from the couch and heading for the kitchen. "Della, you eating with us?"

As Willis followed Glenda into the kitchen, Delphine's eyes darted to the shoes by the door. "No, honey, I've got to get on home to Joe," she said, standing.

"But I do need to use your washroom right quick before I leave."

While Willis's back was turned, Delphine moved quickly, taking the small sewing needle from her purse. She hurried to the kitchen doorway.

"Glenda," she whispered urgently.

Glenda turned from the stove, her face flushed from the steam. Delphine held out the needle. "Quick now. In your mouth. It has to be your spit."

Glenda's face soured with disgust, but seeing the desperate look in her sister's eyes, she took the needle. With a grimace, she put the cold metal in her mouth for just a second, then pulled it out, glistening. Delphine rushed into the other room and picked up one of Willis' shoes.

She hunched over, working the needle's point against the tough rubber of the sole. It was harder to push through than she expected. Her heart pounded against her ribs.

"What you doing with my shoe?"

Willis's voice, casual and curious, cut through the quiet room. Delphine's head snapped up. He had walked back into the sitting room from the kitchen, stopping dead in his tracks to find her hunched over his shoe.

A polite, panicked smile flew to her face. "Oh, this? I was just admiring it. Joe needs a new pair of shoes, and these look real comfortable. Are they?"

From the kitchen doorway, Glenda stood paralyzed, a dish towel twisted in her hands, her face pale. She could see it all happening but could do nothing.

Willis flashed a strange, unreadable smile, his eyes flicking from Delphine to his shoe and back again. "Yeah, they are."

"Where did you get them?" Delphine pressed.

"The shoe shop over on Market Street," he said, his eyes lingering on them for a beat too long. "It's next door to Brown's Haberdashery."

An awkward silence hung in the air.

"Well," Delphine said, placing the shoe back on the floor with deliberate care. "I ought to go get Joe a pair. Anyway, I best be going now." She walked toward the door. Willis stepped out of the way, heading for the bathroom.

Delphine paused at the door and looked back at her sister. Glenda was still standing there, shaking her head almost imperceptibly. Delphine gave her a quick, sharp wink and slipped out into the hallway, leaving Glenda alone with the smell of chicken and dumplings, vinegar, and a desperate, unspoken hope.

Crossing the Line

The first thing Stanley Carr noticed when he woke the next morning was the silence. Not the silence of his small rented room, but the quiet inside his own head. For the first time in several days, the dull, persistent throb that lived behind his eyes was gone. He sat up, swinging his legs over the side of the bed, half-expecting the familiar pain to return with the movement. It didn't. He felt… good.

He reached under the bed and pulled out his work shoes. He turned them over, and four potatoes thudded softly onto the floorboards. He looked at them for a moment, then got dressed, pulling on his work pants but stopping before he put on his undershirt.

He stood bare-chested in front of the small, cracked mirror that hung on his wall. He opened the little vial Dr. Roddie had given him. The scent of rosemary, sharp and clean, filled the air. He poured a small amount of the oil into his palm and began rubbing it onto his chest, his calloused hands working it into the skin. He looked at his own reflection, at the tired eyes that stared back at him.

"I am worthy of a better job," he said, his voice quiet, almost a question. He leaned closer, his eyes locking with the man in the mirror. A new determination burned within him. He said it again, louder this time, his voice firm. "I am worthy of a better job."

He got dressed, grabbed his lunch pail, and walked to the mill.

He went about his day with a new, quiet focus, inspecting pallets, making notes on his clipboard. Around mid-morning, he spotted Mr. Henderson walking the floor. The plant manager stopped to talk with Willis Greene, the new supervisor. Willis was laughing, confident and easy, as Mr. Henderson patted him on the back before moving on.

A familiar wave of discouragement washed over Stanley, cold and bitter. He felt himself shrink back into the shadows of the machinery. But then the words came back to him, a silent mantra in his head. *I am worthy of a better job.* He repeated it to himself, a silent prayer against the roar of the looms.

"What's that?" a coworker beside him asked.

Stanley realized he'd spoken the last part aloud. He just shook his head and, before he could lose his nerve, he started walking toward the plant manager.

Mr. Henderson saw him coming and looked surprised. Stanley was normally meek, a man who blended in with the machinery.

"Mr. Henderson, a word, sir!" Stanley called out, his voice louder than he intended.

Henderson raised an eyebrow. "Yes, Stanley? How are you today?"

"Sir, I've been here for sixteen years," Stanley began, his heart pounding but his voice steady. "I was here when your father ran this place. He was a fine man."

Henderson nodded slowly, his expression unreadable.

"Sir, I feel I'm a good employee, and I'd like to talk to you about advancing. This place is my second home. This is my career. I'd like to move up the ladder. I feel I've earned an opportunity."

There was a long silence. Henderson looked him over, from his worn work boots to his determined eyes, as if seeing him for the first time.

"Stanley," he said finally. "You're right. You've been a solid employee. And my father always spoke very highly of you." He thought for a moment. "Right now, there are no openings. But you've earned more than you're getting." He met Stanley's gaze. "I'm going to give you twenty cents more an hour, starting today. And when something does come open, I will consider you for it."

Stanley was stunned. Twenty cents an hour was a fortune. "Thank you, sir," he managed to say.

Henderson smiled. "No, Stanley. Thank you. Men like you are the reason my family has been successful. I appreciate you."

♦♦♦♦♦♦

On the other side of town, the notes were clunky, the rhythm uncertain, but Alex Jefferson's patience was a deep and steady well. He leaned over the piano, his finger tapping gently on the sheet music. "Now, see that? That's a whole note, Billy. You hold it just a little longer. Try it again."

The little boy, his brow furrowed in concentration, reset his fingers on the keys and plinked out the melody once more. It was better this time.

Alberta walked past the sitting room, a small handbag tucked under her arm. She paused and put a hand on Alex's shoulder, a silent gesture of affection. He looked up and smiled.

She leaned in and whispered, "I'm going down to the market."

Alex nodded as he watched his student. "Alright, darling. Be safe."

Alberta turned and walked to the front door, her mind already making a list: bread, milk, a bit of salt pork if the butcher had any good cuts. She turned the knob and pulled the door open, stepping out into the hallway. As she went to pull the door shut behind her, her eyes caught something on the floor.

A thin, unbroken line of fine gray powder had been laid across her threshold, just in front of the welcome mat.

She froze, her hand still on the doorknob. It was so neat, so deliberate. She leaned down, squinting to get a better look. It looked like ash. *Strange,* she thought. She let the door close and walked down the hall to the next apartment, her footsteps soft on the runner. Nothing. She walked the entire length of the second-floor hallway, checking in front of every door. Only hers.

Her wheels were turning, connecting this strange powder to the voodoo practitioner downstairs. What was the powder? What did it mean? A wave of nausea rolled through her stomach.

She got downstairs and pushed through the heavy front door into the bright afternoon light. The feeling of sickness intensified. She made it to the edge of the parking lot before her body rebelled, and she doubled over, vomiting into the weeds by the curb.

"Mrs. Jefferson? Are you alright?" A neighbor from the first floor, Mrs. McNamee, rushed over, her face etched with concern.

Alberta, feeling faint and humiliated, waved her off. "I'm fine," she managed to say, wiping her mouth with a handkerchief from her purse. "Just... just something I ate."

She slowly walked back up the stairs to her

apartment, her hand gripping the wooden railing for support. Each step was a monumental effort. She paused on the landing below her own, her eyes fixed on Dr. Roddie's door for a long, hard moment. The wood seemed to pulse with a dark energy.

Struggling up the final flight of stairs, she finally reached her own door, the gray line of ash waiting like a serpent. As she reached for the knob, a wave of dizziness washed over her, and her legs gave out. She crumpled to the floor.

"Help!" she cried out, her voice thin and desperate. "Alex, help me!"

The piano stopped abruptly. The door flew open, and Alex rushed out. "Bertie! What is it? What's wrong?" He helped her to her knees.

She didn't answer, just stopped and pointed a trembling finger at the floor. "What is that?"

Alex looked down, his expression perplexed. "What, the dust? Honey, I'm not sure…"

He helped her inside, closing the door behind them. He guided her to a chair and rushed to get her a glass of water. The little boy, Billy, stood stunned by the piano, his eyes wide with fear.

"Everything is fine, son," Alex said, his voice a little shaky. "I'll be right back."

He knelt beside Alberta's chair, handing her the water. As she took it, he suddenly dropped the glass, which shattered on the floor. He fell to one knee, his hand clutching at the center of his chest.

Alberta's eyes widened in horror. "Oh, no. Alex!"

He collapsed onto the floor, his breath coming in ragged gasps. Alberta looked from her husband to the terrified student.

"Young man, you stay right there! Don't you move! I'll be right back."

Alberta, ignoring her own weakness, slowly made her way out into the hall and down the two flights of stairs again, her knuckles white on the railing. She got down to the first floor and banged on door 101.

"Felix! Felix, open the door!"

A moment later, the door opened, and a man in his seventies with a tired, craggy face appeared. "What's wrong, Alberta? What's all the shouting?"

"We need help! It's Alex, he's on the floor! Call the hospital! We ain't got no phone."

Felix Acres' eyes nearly popped out of his head. He rushed over to a small table where a black rotary phone sat. He snatched the receiver and dialed until he got an operator.

"We need an ambulance at the Riverside Apartments on North Central. Right away!" He slammed the phone back down. "Help is on the way," he said, his voice trembling slightly.

When Alberta got back to her apartment, Alex had managed to pull himself into a chair. He was doubled over, his face pale and slick with sweat, still clutching his chest in agony. Within a few minutes medical personnel were on the scene to take Alex to the hospital.

♦♦♦♦♦♦

The narrow stairwell groaned under the weight of the men from the city hospital. They navigated the stretcher with practiced, heavy steps, a grim expression on their faces. Alex Jefferson lay on the stretcher, pale and still, his eyes closed in a mask of pain. Behind them, a shaken Felix Acres helped Alberta down the stairs, her sobs echoing in the enclosed space.

As they reached the first-floor landing, the front door of the building opened. A well-dressed woman with a pleasant, expectant smile stepped inside, pausing to let her eyes adjust to the dim hallway. Her smile vanished, replaced by a look of shock as she took in the scene before her.

"Oh, my goodness! What's happened?" she asked, her voice laced with alarm.

"Medical emergency, ma'am," Felix said gruffly, focused on helping a stumbling Alberta. "Please, we need to get through."

The woman's eyes widened with a new, personal fear. "My son," she said, her voice rising slightly. "Billy? He's upstairs for his piano lesson with Mr. Jefferson."

Alberta looked at the woman with tear-filled, unseeing eyes, the words barely registering through the fog of her own terror. The paramedics maneuvered the stretcher around the newel post and out the front door.

"The apartment door is open," Felix called back to the worried mother over his shoulder. "You can go on up and get him."

Billy's mother stood frozen for a moment in the now-empty hall, listening to the sounds of the ambulance doors closing outside before she gathered herself and hurried nervously up the stairs.

Just as Alberta and Felix reached the front door, Lizzie Roddie stepped inside, carrying a small cardboard box of groceries. She stopped dead, her eyes widening at the chaotic scene before her.

Alberta's head whipped around, her face streaked with tears, her eyes wild with grief and rage. Her gaze locked with Lizzie's.

"Your husband did this!" Alberta shrieked, her voice raw and ragged.

Lizzie, stunned, took a half-step back. The box tilted in her arms. "Uh, ma'am... What's going on?"

"Come on, Mrs. Jefferson,"Felix said gently, ushering her toward the open door where the ambulance waited, its red light painting a silent, pulsing rhythm on the walls. The paramedics helped her inside and began to close the heavy doors. But before they shut, Alberta lunged forward one last time.

"He's of the devil!" she screamed, her voice muffled as the doors slammed shut.

The words hung in the air, more shocking than any siren. Lizzie stood frozen for a moment, then, with a new urgency, rushed up the stairs. She didn't stop at her own door but continued to the second floor, peering through the Jeffersons' still-open doorway. Inside, she saw the little boy who had been at the piano. His mother was kneeling before him, wrapping him in a fierce, protective hug as he sobbed into her shoulder. The sight of the terrified child sent a chill through Lizzie's spine. She backed away from the door and hurried back down to her own apartment.

She burst through her own front door. "Obie?"

The apartment was quiet. She rushed through the house, her heart pounding, and threw back the beaded curtain to the conjure room. It was empty, the air still and heavy with the scent of old smoke. She turned and went into the sitting room and stopped.

He was there. Obie sat in his favorite armchair by the window, his eyes closed, a look of serene contentment on his face. The radio on the table beside him was playing softly. Frank Sinatra's smooth voice filled the room.

Give me five minutes more, only five minutes more…

Lizzie stood in the doorway, breathless. Obie's eyes fluttered open, and he smiled when he saw her.

"Now this is music," he said, his voice a low, pleasant hum. "Mr. Sinatra stirs the soul."

Lizzie studied him, searching his calm face for any sign of guilt or agitation. She found none. "Obie… what did you do?"

He gave her a strange, quizzical look. "What do you mean, dear?"

"The Jeffersons," she said, her voice trembling slightly. "They were just loaded into an ambulance. Obie, the man was on a stretcher. Mrs. Jefferson… she screamed at me. She said some awful things."

Roddie smirked, a small, knowing expression, and turned his attention back to the radio.

Lizzie stepped further into the room. "Did you do something?"

He pondered the question for a second, his head tilted as if considering the weight of it. "I… I just want them to feel unwelcome here, that's all," he said finally, his tone reasonable. "There's a thing called common courtesy. That family seems to lack it."

There was a pause. He looked at her, his eyes clear and steady. "When you came home just now, did you hear Mr. Sinatra as you came up the stairs?"

Lizzie, confused, shook her head. "No."

"Now then," he said with an air of finality. "I am a good neighbor."

She stared at him, perplexed, trying to make sense of his twisted logic. He turned away from her as the song ended and another began. Perry Como's voice filled the room.

I'm just a prisoner of love...

Roddie pointed a finger at the radio. "This is a good one, too."

Lizzie didn't answer. She backed away slowly and walked into the kitchen, the sound of the crooning following her. She set her groceries on the counter, her hands shaking, not knowing what to think, or what to fear more: the woman screaming in the ambulance, or the calm, smiling man in the other room.

♦♦♦♦♦♦

The hospital room was quiet, save for the soft, rhythmic puff of an oxygen tank and the faint rustle of starched sheets. Alex lay on the high metal bed, a thin blanket pulled up to his chest, his face pale and slack. He was barely coherent, his eyes closed, his breathing shallow. An IV stand stood beside the bed, a glass bottle dripping a slow, steady lifeline into his arm. The medical equipment felt primitive, unequal to the task.

The doctor, a man with tired eyes and a kind but clinical demeanor, folded his arms. "His heart took a real strain, Mrs. Jefferson. What we call a myocardial infarction. This is serious."

He paused, seeing the confusion on her face. "A heart attack. He's a lucky man to have gotten here so quickly. But he's getting to that age. He needs to take better care of himself, watch his diet, avoid stress."

Just then, the door opened quietly, and a young woman peered in, her face stricken. "Auntie Bertie?"

It was their niece, Chantelle. She was twenty-five,

with kind eyes, which were now welling with tears. Alberta rushed to her and pulled her into a tight hug.

"I came as soon as I heard," Chantelle whispered into her aunt's shoulder.

Alberta held her for a moment, then turned back to the doctor, her expression hardening. "This wasn't about his diet, Doctor."

The doctor raised an eyebrow. "I'm sorry?"

"Does he have a history of heart trouble in his family?" he asked. "His father, his mother?"

"No," Alberta said firmly. "They are both still alive, up in their seventies, and in perfect health. This wasn't natural." She took a deep breath, her voice low but clear. "It was voodoo."

The doctor's professional mask slipped. A short, sharp laugh escaped before he could disguise it as a cough. He looked away, embarrassed. Chantelle, however, just stared at her aunt with a strange, worried look.

"Mrs. Jefferson," the doctor said, recovering his composure. "Your husband has a serious medical condition. Our focus right now needs to be on his recovery." He patted her arm condescendingly. "I have to see to my other patients, but I'll be back to check on him in a little while." He gave a curt nod and exited the room.

Chantelle gently guided her aunt to a small vinyl chair by the window. "Auntie, are you alright? You look pale."

"I got violently ill earlier today," Alberta confided, her voice a low murmur. "Right before Alex... right before this happened."

Before Chantelle could respond, another figure appeared in the doorway. It was Reverend Thompson from their church, his large frame filling the space, his face a mask of solemn concern.

"Sister Alberta," he said, his voice a comforting baritone. "I came as quick as I could. How is he?"

"It's his heart, Reverend," she said, her own heart aching with the word.

The reverend stepped further into the room and placed a comforting hand on her shoulder. "May I pray with you? For Alex?"

"Yes," Alberta said, her eyes blazing with a desperate fire. "Please. Pray for Alex… and pray for our family. We need protection from evil."

Reverend Thompson gave her a strange look, his brow furrowing slightly at her specific, urgent plea. He glanced at Chantelle, who returned his look with one of her own, a shared, silent expression of concern for the woman between them.

The three of them joined hands around Alex's bedside. The Reverend's deep voice filled the sterile room.

"O Lord, our Heavenly Father," he began, his eyes closed tightly. "We come before you today with heavy hearts, asking for your grace and your mercy to fall upon this room. We lift up our brother Alex to you. We ask you, in your infinite wisdom, to lay your healing hand upon him. Soothe his pain, Lord, mend what has been afflicted, and grant his body the strength and fortitude to recover from this trial."

As his voice rose with passion, Alberta bowed her head and prayed harder than she ever had in her life—but her prayer was a silent, desperate scream. She wasn't asking for peace; she was asking for a sword. She wasn't praying for healing; she was praying for vengeance. She prayed for the Lord to build a wall of fire around her family, strong enough to keep the devil downstairs at bay.

The Law

The Knoxville police station smelled of stale cigarette smoke and floor polish. Alberta Jefferson sat on a hard wooden bench, her back straight, her hands clutching her purse in her lap. She had been waiting for twenty minutes, watching officers move with a purpose that felt both urgent and deeply routine. A typewriter clacked incessantly from a back office, its rhythm occasionally matched by the soft whir of a large oscillating fan that swept a meager breeze across the room. She was trying to be patient, to present her case with the calm dignity it deserved.

A young officer with a clean-shaven face and kind eyes approached her. "Mrs. Jefferson? I'm Officer Miller. You can come on back."

She followed him to a small wooden desk cluttered with papers. He gestured for her to sit. "Now, how can I help you?"

Alberta took a deep breath. "I need to file a report, Officer. Against my neighbor, Mr. Obie Roddie."

The officer picked up a pen. "And what is the nature of the complaint?"

"He's threatening my family," she began, her voice steady at first. "He put a strange powder, looked like ashes, in a line across the threshold of my front door."

Officer Miller paused his writing, looking up with a perplexed expression. "A powder?"

"Yes," she insisted. "And as soon as I saw it, I got sick. And then… then my husband, Alex, he collapsed. He had a heart attack." Her composure began to crack, her voice rising with emotion. "It was because of that powder. He tried to kill him!"

"Ma'am..."

"And that's not all," she said, leaning forward, her voice dropping to a conspiratorial whisper. "He was behind that fire on Gay Street. The one that killed the real estate man. I know it."

The young officer held up a placating hand. "Mrs. Jefferson, hold on a moment. Let me check something." He stood and walked over to a tall metal filing cabinet, the drawer protesting with a loud screech as he pulled it open. He thumbed through a series of manila folders before pulling one out. He returned to his desk, opened the folder, and scanned the top page.

He looked up at her, his expression now one of professional finality. "Ma'am, I have the fire marshal's report right here. The official cause of the fire at the real estate office was determined to be faulty electrical wiring. There was no foul play suspected."

Alberta stared at him, her face twisting into a dirty look of pure disbelief.

The officer sighed, trying one last time to appeal to reason. He held the open folder out across the desk to her. "Would you like to see the report, ma'am?"

She scowled and shook her head sharply, refusing to even look at the paper in front of her.

He closed the folder with a soft thud. "I understand you're upset. But there's no evidence of a crime here. And as for your neighbor..."

Alberta grimaced.

"Unless he walks in here and confesses to trying to poison you, I can't do a thing about it."

Alberta stared at him, her mouth wide open. The casual dismissal, the faint hint of humor in his voice, felt like a slap. All her fear, her certainty, her terror—it all amounted to nothing in this room. The law could not see what she saw.

She pushed her chair back abruptly, its legs scraping loudly against the wooden floor. The sound made another officer look up from his typing.

"You're no help," she said, her voice dripping with a cold fury. "No help at all."

She turned and stormed out of the station, pushing through the heavy doors and back into the afternoon sun. The city hummed around her—trolleys rattling, people laughing, life moving on as if nothing was wrong. But everything was wrong. The doctor wouldn't listen. The police wouldn't listen. She was completely, utterly alone in this fight, and the chilling realization settled in her soul like a stone.

♦♦♦♦♦♦

Alberta Jefferson returned to the apartment complex on foot, the walk from the bus stop leaving her weary and drained. As she cut through the parking lot, a car pulled in. A well-dressed woman she didn't recognize got out and retrieved a pie from the back seat, carefully balancing the pastry box in her hands. The warm scent of baked apples and cinnamon drifted across the asphalt. Alberta walked past without a word, heading for the landlord's office on the first floor.

She knocked firmly on the door to apartment 101.

Felix Acres opened it, his tired face softening when he saw her. "Alberta. Come in, come in."

She stepped into his small, cluttered office, which smelled of old paper and pipe tobacco, and took a seat in the chair opposite his desk.

"How's Alex feeling?" Felix asked, his voice full of genuine concern.

"He came home from the hospital yesterday," she said, her voice flat. "He's resting. Hardly sleeps."

"Well, I've been keeping him in my prayers," Felix said. He leaned forward, his elbows on the desk. "Is there anything at all I can do to help?"

Alberta seized the opening. "Yes, Felix. There is." She sat up straighter, her eyes locked on his. "I want you to kick that voodoo man out. I want him gone."

The landlord looked baffled. "Obie Roddie? The fella in 203?"

"He's in league with the devil," she said, her voice low and intense. "He is behind all of Alex's health problems. He put some kind of evil voodoo hex on our door."

Felix stared at her, then a disbelieving smile tugged at the corner of his mouth. He tried to hide it but couldn't. He shook his head. "Alberta, Mr. Roddie and his wife have been perfect tenants. They've been here for six months and have never missed a rent payment. In fact, they pay a week early, every time."

"I don't care if they pay a year early," she snapped.

"I'm sorry, Alberta, but I can't just evict a man for... for what you're describing," Felix said gently. "Have you tried talking to them? They're actually very nice people. I don't think they'd do anything to harm anyone."

Alberta's face hardened into a mask of cold fury. The final door had just closed. The law, the doctors, and now the landlord—no one would help her. "I best be going," she said, her voice clipped.

She stood and stormed toward the door.

"Alberta, please," Felix called out after her, his voice full of concern. "Come back over here and talk to me."

She didn't slow down. Her hand was on the doorknob.

"Alberta!" he called again, more urgently this time.

She pulled the door open and stepped out into the hall without looking back, leaving a completely baffled Felix Acres shaking his head in her wake.

She marched up the stairs, her anger a hot coal in her chest. As she reached the second-floor landing, she heard a soft *click*—the sound of Roddie's door closing. She hadn't seen him, only the ghost of his presence. Her skin crawled.

She continued up to her own floor and stopped, staring at the faint gray line of ash still marking her threshold. With a huff, she unlocked her door, went straight to the kitchen closet, and grabbed the broom and dustpan. She returned to the hallway and began sweeping the ashes into a corner with furious, jerky motions, puffing with rage. After she had swept every last trace of the powder into the pan, she held it away from her body as if it were a venomous snake, pinching her nose shut with her free hand. She would not have this evil dust near her home.

She marched down the two flights of stairs, out the front door, and around the corner into the alley behind the hardware store. She dumped the entire dustpan into a large metal trashcan with a loud, satisfying clang, then hurried away, not wanting to breathe the air anywhere near it.

By the time she walked back up the stairs, the anger had drained out of her, leaving only a vast, hollow exhaustion. She let herself quietly into the apartment. She gathered a suitcase full of clothes for herself and Alex and then went back downstairs to begin the long walk back to the bus stop.

♦♦♦♦♦♦

A few hours later, Alberta entered Alex's room in the hospital carrying the suitcase. In the dim light of the room, a figure looked up from a chair. It was Chantelle, a book resting in her lap.

The young woman put a single finger to her lips. "Shhhh...," she whispered. "Uncle Alex is sleeping."

Alberta nodded, her heart aching with gratitude for her niece's presence. "You go on home now, child," she whispered back, her voice full of a soft authority. "You can come back tomorrow. Go home and get some rest."

Chantelle stood and stretched, a wide yawn escaping her lips. "Okay, Auntie Alberta."

Alberta pulled her niece into a firm hug. "I love you," she said. "You're a blessing."

After Chantelle had quietly gathered her things and left, Alberta was finally alone with her husband. She walked over to his bedside and knelt on the cold floor, placing both of her hands on his sleeping form. He looked so pale, so fragile. She bowed her head and began to pray, her whispers emphatic and fierce, pleading with God to heal him and to protect their family from the dark, relentless forces in their apartment building that were closing in.

♦♦♦♦♦♦

The next morning, a polite knock sounded at the Roddie's' apartment door. Lizzie opened it to find Delphine Tucker standing in the hallway, holding a pie with both hands. A rich, warm scent of baked blueberries wafted into the apartment.

"Mrs. Tucker!" Lizzie said, her face breaking into a wide, welcoming smile. "My, that smells wonderful. Please, come in."

As Delphine stepped inside, Roddie appeared from the conjure room. His eyes landed on the pie. "Is that blueberry?" he asked, a grin spreading across his face. "That smells delicious."

He gently took the pie from Delphine and handed it to Lizzie, who took it to the kitchen as if it were a precious jewel. Roddie then gestured for Delphine to follow him back through the beaded curtain.

They sat in their usual spots. "Thank you for that pie, Mrs. Tucker, but you shouldn't have," he said warmly. "Now, what can I do for you today?"

Delphine beamed, her face alight with a joy that made her look ten years younger. "Nothing, Dr. Roddie. I don't need a thing. I came to thank you. Everything worked. And it's even better than my sister could have ever imagined."

Roddie leaned back, a look of deep satisfaction on his face. "Is that so?"

"She did everything you asked of her," Delphine recounted, her words tumbling out in her excitement. "The coffee, vinegar, the shoe. All of it. Willis got that promotion at the mill, the one he'd been hoping for! More money, better hours, everything. Then, yesterday, he took her on a picnic down by the river and he asked her to marry him."

Roddie chuckled, a warm, genuine sound. "Well, I trust she said yes."

Delphine laughed. "Of course, she did! She was so happy she was crying. We both were. In just a few months, my sister will be Mrs. Willis Greene."

Roddie's smile widened. "I like the sound of that," he said. "That is wonderful news. I am so happy for her. For both of you. And for Mr. Greene."

"I just had to bring you a pie and tell you the good news myself," Delphine said, her eyes shining with gratitude. "You are an angel, Dr. Roddie. Truly doing the Lord's work."

"You are too kind, Mrs. Tucker," he said with a humble nod.

Delphine stood, smoothing her dress. "You go on and enjoy that pie, honey."

He thanked her again and saw her to the door. After she left, Roddie went into the kitchen. He found Lizzie sitting at the small table, flipping through a book. He smiled when he saw the small, faint blue smudge at the corner of her mouth.

He started to laugh.

She looked up, puzzled. "What's so funny?"

He couldn't help himself. "How is the pie?"
Lizzie's expression turned sheepish. "How did you know?" she asked, dabbing at her mouth with a napkin.

He pointed to the pie tin sitting on the counter. A single, neat indentation marked the edge of the golden crust where Lizzie had taken a small bite directly from the pie. He laughed again, a full, happy sound that filled the small kitchen. He went to the cabinet, got two plates and two forks, and brought the pie to the table, setting it down between them. As he cut the first proper slice, the warm, sweet filling spilling onto the plate, the troubles of the world—and the quiet, simmering war with the neighbors upstairs—seemed, for a moment, very far away.

♦♦♦♦♦♦

A few days after Alex returned home from the hospital, the apartment had taken on the quiet, tense atmosphere of a sickroom. Alex spent most of his time resting in bed, his strength slow to return, leaving Alberta and Chantelle to tiptoe around the rooms and speak in hushed whispers.

Alberta was folding a blanket in the sitting room when a soft knock came at the door.

She opened it to find Edna Gable standing in the hallway, a look of gentle concern on her face.

Alberta's expression was flat and cold. "I think you're on the wrong floor."

Edna shook her head, a small, knowing laugh escaping her lips. "No, Alberta. I came to see you. I heard your husband wasn't well."

The sincerity in her voice was undeniable. Alberta sighed and stepped back, opening the door wider. "Come in."

They sat in the small sitting room. Just as Edna was about to speak, the bedroom door creaked open and Chantelle emerged, closing it quietly behind her.

"He's finally resting," she whispered.

"Chantelle, this is an old friend of mine, Edna Gable. Edna, my niece, Chantelle."

"It's nice to meet you," Edna said warmly.

Chantelle returned the smile. "You as well. Auntie Alberta, I'm going to head on home now. I've got a mountain of laundry to do."

Alberta stood and pulled her niece into a tight hug. "Thank you, honey. For all you do."

After Chantelle left, an awkward silence settled in the room. Edna could feel her friend's tension like a physical wall between them. "Alberta, what's wrong?"

Alberta looked at her, her eyes hard. "I've known you a long time, Edna. I care about you. But I need to know. What is your relationship with Mr. Roddie downstairs?"

Edna's composure faltered. She looked down at her hands. "I just... I sought out some advice. I needed a different perspective. My husband... Douglas wasn't showing me any affection."

Alberta reached over to the small table beside her chair and picked up the heavy family Bible, its leather cover worn smooth with time. She held it up. "A different perspective? Edna, all the perspective you or any other soul needs is right in here."

Edna nodded, not meeting her gaze. "Yes, yes, I know." There was a long pause. When Edna looked up, her eyes were swimming with tears. "Alberta... he was cheating on me."

The confession hung in the air, raw and painful. Alberta's hard expression softened instantly. She hung her head, ashamed of her own righteousness. Finally, she looked up. "Edna, I'm sorry," she said, her voice full of genuine sympathy. "I truly am. But still... that man is dabbling in some dark stuff. You best not fool with that stuff." She leaned forward, her voice dropping to a whisper. "You went to him for help and..." she paused, letting the implication hang in the air, "...well, now you're a widow."

"Alberta, I know you feel strongly about this," Edna said, shaking her head. "But Dr. Roddie only tried to help me."

"You best stay away from him," Alberta insisted, her conviction returning. "That man is evil. I came home the other day and there was some kind of powder in a line in front of my door. It made me sick. And not twenty minutes later, Alex had his heart attack."

Edna challenged her gently. "Maybe it was just dust from the hallway, Alberta."

"It was not dust."

"And you said you got sick?" Edna continued. "Maybe you got some food poisoning. And you and your husband, well... you're getting older. Maybe you should just cut back on fatty foods, eat a little better."

"Are you saying this is my fault?" Alberta asked, her voice rising with anger.

"No, of course not," Edna said, trying to smooth things over. She reached out and took Alberta's hand. "I don't mean to offend. I care about you. I only came by to see if you needed anything. How about I bring y'all supper tomorrow night?"

Alberta pulled her hand away, but the anger in her eyes had softened slightly. "That's kind of you, Edna, but our preacher is coming over tomorrow night."

Edna smiled, picking up on the hint. She stood to leave. "I understand. Well... how about we get coffee sometime soon?"

A small, genuine smile finally cracked Alberta's somber face. "I'd like that."

Edna gave her friend a brief, warm hug and walked out. As soon as the door closed, Alberta opened it a crack, peering into the hallway. She watched Edna descend the stairs. On the second-floor landing, Edna paused. She turned and looked at Dr. Roddie's door for a long moment. Then, she shook her head almost imperceptibly, turned away, and continued down the stairs and out of the building.

Rock of Ages

A few days later, a fragile hope began to return to the Jefferson apartment. Alex was stirring, moving with a slowness that felt more like recovery than infirmity. With his niece, Chantelle, walking dutifully alongside him, he made his way from the bedroom into the kitchen and poured himself a glass of water, his hand only trembling slightly.

Alberta watched him from the doorway, a genuine smile touching her lips for the first time in what felt like an eternity. "You're looking better. You've got some color back."

He took a long drink, the water cool against his throat. He let out a deep breath and nodded. "I'm feeling more like myself," he said, and his voice had a hint of its old strength.

Chantelle's face lit up. "Uncle Alex… do you think you could play me a song on the piano?"

His eyes, which had been dull with pain and medication, sparked with their old light. "Well now," he said, a slow grin spreading across his face. "I suppose I'm up to playing a little tune."

He shuffled over to the piano, each step a small victory. He settled onto the bench, his fingers hovering over the keys for a moment before landing on a familiar, jaunty little riff. He laughed, a real, hearty sound that filled the room.

"Ah, yeah," he said, playing it again. "Feels good."

"It sounds wonderful, darling," Alberta chimed in from the kitchen doorway, her heart swelling.

Chantelle slid onto the bench beside him, her eyes

sparkling. "Oh, Uncle Alex, play that Bing Crosby song I like!"

Alex chuckled, his fingers finding a bouncy, optimistic rhythm on the keys. "Which one's that?"

"You know!" she urged. "'Pennies from Heaven'!"

He laughed and began to plink out the intro, but before he could start in earnest, Alberta's voice came from the doorway, gentle but firm.

"No, honey," she said, looking straight at her husband. "Play 'Rock of Ages' for me."

The lighthearted mood in the room shifted instantly. Alex looked at his wife and saw the deep, unwavering plea in her eyes. This wasn't a casual request; it was a need. He nodded slowly, and his hands moved from the jaunty tune to the solid, comforting chords of the old hymn.

As he played, Chantelle's clear, sweet voice rose to join the music, and soon Alex began to hum along, his baritone a low, rumbling harmony. They played and sang loudly, their joy now infused with a sense of solemn purpose—a defiant proclamation against the sickness and fear that had haunted the apartment. The music poured out of the sitting room, a powerful, life-affirming sound, filling every corner with a melody of hope and healing.

♦♦♦♦♦♦

The clatter of plates and hum of conversation at the S&W Cafeteria felt a world away from the roar of the Brookside Mills office. Willis Greene sat opposite the plant manager, Mr. Henderson, a plate of meatloaf and gravy before him, a wide, confident grin on his face.

"So, how are you liking the new role?" Henderson

asked, taking a sip of water. "Everything you hoped for?"

"It's better, sir," Willis said, glowing with pride. "I love it. It's a challenge, but I feel like I was born for it."

When the waitress came by, Henderson ordered a whiskey with his meal. "A little celebration," he said with a wink. "Willis?"

Against his better judgment—he never drank in the middle of a workday—Willis nodded. "I'll have the same."

The first drink warmed him, a pleasant burn that settled deep in his gut. When the waitress returned to the table, she smiled. "Can I get you gentlemen another?"

"No, I'm fine," Mr. Henderson said, placing a hand over his half-empty glass. "We've got a factory to run." He looked to Willis.

"I'll have another," Willis said eagerly, perhaps a little too quickly.

Henderson raised an eyebrow, a flicker of surprise in his expression. "You sure?"

Willis, feeling bold and wanting to project an air of relaxed confidence, waved off the concern. "Absolutely. We haven't been to lunch since my promotion. Why not have a proper celebration?"

The waitress nodded and left. The second whiskey arrived, and as Willis took the first sip, the warmth spread through his veins, bolstering his already high spirits. He felt invincible.

Back at the mill that afternoon, the warmth of the whiskey had settled into a dull haze. Willis strode across the floor, his walk a little too loose, his voice a little too loud. He grabbed a clipboard with a large shipping manifest for an order of flour, giving it only a cursory glance before initialing the bottom.

"Alright boys, load it up!" he shouted over the noise. "Get all twenty-two pallets on the truck for the delivery to Quality Foods!"

An older worker looked up from the manifest in his own hands, his brow furrowed in confusion. "Twenty-two pallets, sir? The order here says two."

Willis snatched the paper from the man's hand and squinted at it, the small type swimming slightly. He saw the number two, but his overconfident, whiskey-addled brain registered it as a typo. "I know what the order is," he snapped, handing it back. "It's twenty-two. Get it on the truck."

An hour later, Mr. Henderson came storming out of his office, his face the color of a thundercloud. "Willis! My office. Now."

As Willis walked toward the office, the same worker who had questioned him muttered to a friend, just loud enough for Willis to hear, "He's drunk."

Henderson closed the office door behind them. The silence was deafening after the noise of the floor.

"I had a call from the loading dock, Willis," the manager said, his voice cold and even. "Then I had another call from one of your men. Everyone on that floor knows you've been drinking. I can smell it on you from here. I gave you a chance, a big one. And you threw it away." He shook his head in disgust. "I have to let you go. Clean out your locker."

The words hit Willis like a punch to the gut. He opened his mouth to argue, to explain, but no sound came out. He just nodded, turned, and walked out of the office in a daze.

As he stepped back onto the main floor, his dreams in ruins, his gaze fell on Stanley Carr. The older man was diligently checking a pallet of flour, his movements steady and focused, the picture of a reliable worker.

Mr. Henderson stood in his office doorway, watching Willis's walk of shame. His eyes followed Willis's and landed on Stanley, too. The problem was leaving; the solution was right in front of him.

"Mr. Carr!" Henderson barked. "My office." Stanley looked up, startled. He wiped his hands on a rag and nervously walked to the office. Mr. Henderson gestured for him to come inside and shut the door.

"Stanley," the manager said, getting straight to the point. "A while back, you came to me and said you wanted more responsibility. Do you still feel that way?"

Stanley's heart began to pound. He could feel the faint, slick residue of the rosemary oil on his chest, a secret shield of confidence. "Yes, sir," he said, his voice clear and steady. "I do."

"Good," Henderson said with a decisive nod. "The supervisor position is open again. It's yours if you want it. It's fifty dollars a week."

Fifty dollars a week. The number was so large it barely seemed real. It was more than he had ever dreamed of making. All he could see was Dr. Roddie's knowing smile. All he could feel was a wave of overwhelming gratitude.

He eagerly extended his hand. "Yes, sir," Stanley said, his voice thick with emotion. "I'll take it. I won't let you down.

Willis Greene walked, the shame of his firing a hot, heavy stone in his gut. He replayed Mr. Henderson's cold, final words over and over in his mind. Each step toward Glenda's house felt like a mile. How could he tell her? How could he look at her face, so full of hope for their future, and tell her that he had ruined it all in a single afternoon?

He was a block away from her house when the sign of a corner tavern caught his eye. He paused, telling himself he just needed one beer to clear his head, to find the right words. He pushed through the door into the dim, smoky bar.

One beer didn't provide the courage he needed, nor did the second. By the time he slapped a few coins down for the third, the shame had been replaced by a bitter, liquid confidence. Now he had the nerve.

He knocked on Glenda's door. She opened it, her face breaking into a bright, surprised smile. "Willis! Honey, what are you doing here?"

"I have something to tell you," he said, his words a little thick.

"Oh?" she said, her eyes alight with excitement. "Did you find a church? The one with the pretty steeple over on Main Street?"

"Not exactly," he stammered, stalling.

She leaned in to kiss him, then pulled back, her nose wrinkled. "Willis… you smell like a bar." Her tone shifted from happy to concerned. "What is it? What's wrong?"

He got defensive. "Can't a man have a beer after a long day?"

"What's going on?" she pressed, her voice firmer now.

He finally looked at her, the bravado draining from his face. "I lost my job," he mumbled.

"What?" Her hand flew to her mouth. "What do you mean, you lost your job?"

"It doesn't matter," he insisted, stepping further into the room. "We can still get married. It'll be fine."

"Fine?" she said, her voice rising in disbelief. "How will we afford a wedding? A life? I can barely afford this little place on my salary."

"I don't know!" he said, his own anger flaring. "I can move in here with you for a while."

"What did you do, Willis?" she asked, her voice sharp.

"It wasn't my fault! I made a simple mistake!"

"A simple mistake that cost you your new promotion? Were you drunk?"

The accusation hit him like a physical blow. "Don't you talk to me like that!" he snarled.

She pressed further, stepping toward him, her own anger overriding her fear. "I'll talk to you how I please! Were you drinking on the job?"

He snapped. His hand flew out and smacked her across the cheek.

The crack of the slap echoed in the small room, shocking them both into a sudden, horrifying silence. Glenda stared at him, her eyes wide with disbelief, her hand slowly rising to touch her stinging face. Willis looked at his own hand as if it belonged to a stranger.

"Uh… Glenda, I'm sorry," he stammered, taking a step toward her. "I didn't mean…"

Her expression hardened into something cold and absolute. "Get out," she said, her voice low and trembling with rage.

"Honey, I..."

"Get out!" she screamed, pointing a shaking finger at the door. "Get out and don't you ever come back! I wouldn't marry you if you were the last man in Knoxville!"

He slowly backpedaled, his face a mask of confusion and regret. "I'm sorry," he whispered one last time. "I didn't mean it."

He turned and left, pulling the door shut behind him. For a long moment, Glenda stood perfectly still in the center of her living room. Then, her legs gave out, and she sank onto the couch and buried her face in her hands, her body shaking with deep, wrenching sobs.

♦♦♦♦♦♦

Roddie was in the kitchen, leaning against the counter while Lizzie wiped it down. "You know, when this next month is covered, we should take a trip," he said, a rare, relaxed smile on his face. "Just the two of us. Down to Florida, maybe. You deserve a nice vacation."

"Oh, Obie, that sounds..."

She was cut off by the faint, but unmistakable, sound of piano music starting up from the floor above. Roddie groaned and rolled his eyes, the pleasant moment shattered.

Before he could say a word, a frantic, desperate knocking rattled their front door.

He opened it to find Delphine Tucker, but she was not the grateful client who had brought him a pie. Her face was streaked with tears, her hat was askew, and her eyes burned with a furious fire.

"Mrs. Tucker?" he said, stunned.

He ushered her into the conjure room and they sat. Before he could ask what was wrong, she unleashed her story.

"He hit her, Dr. Roddie!" she cried, her voice cracking. "Willis got fired from that new job at the mill, went off and got drunk, and when he showed up at Glenda's, he smacked her right across the face! The wedding is off. Everything is ruined!"

Roddie stared, unable to speak. He felt the blood drain from his face. "How... how is your sister?"

"She's heartbroken," Delphine sobbed. "She finally found some happiness, and now this."

Roddie sank down in his chair and put his head in his hands, the gravity of her words pressing down on him. This wasn't possible. He thought for a long, silent moment, then sat up straight. "Okay," he said, his voice quiet. "Okay."

He got up and walked to a box on the cabinet, pouring a small amount of fine, black gunpowder into a glass vial. He walked back out to the kitchen. Lizzie looked up, surprised, as he reached into the refrigerator and pulled out a fresh lemon. He returned to the conjure room, his focus absolute.

He set the items on the table. "Tell Glenda to sprinkle this gunpowder on her body before she goes to bed, and then spritz it with this lemon juice," he said, his voice regaining its professional calm. He handed her the lemon and the vial. "This will reunite them."

Delphine frowned, shaking her head. "Dr. Roddie, she doesn't want him back. Not after this."

Roddie scratched his head, genuinely perplexed. As he tried to think, the sound of the piano upstairs seemed to mock him, each note a small, clunky reminder of his irritation. He glared at the ceiling, his frustration boiling over. He snapped his gaze back to Delphine, a new theory dawning in his eyes.

"It sounds like Willis and Glenda are cursed," he said, the idea taking shape as he spoke. He grabbed a fresh piece of paper and began scribbling frantically. "Here's what Glenda needs to do. She must get a handkerchief, tie it into three knots, and dip it in dirty water. Once it's completely dried, she must place it in her pocket. This will repel the negative influences… reverse them, actually. It puts a stop to whatever is working against them."

He pushed the paper into her hand. "Here, I wrote it all down for you. This should stop the dark forces working against Glenda and her fiancée. Perhaps their luck will change after this."

Delphine took the paper, her expression apprehensive.

"Mrs. Tucker," he said, his voice now soft and sincere. "I want things to be right for your sister. Please, there is no charge today. Go. I hope this will make things right."

Delphine looked at him, at the genuine distress in his eyes, and her frustration finally softened. She squeezed his arm. "Thank you, Doctor."

As soon as the door clicked shut behind Delphine Tucker, the sound of the piano from upstairs seemed to rush in to fill the void, each note a tiny hammer blow against Dr. Roddie's frayed composure. The confusion and shock from Delphine's visit curdled instantly into pure, hot rage.

He moved to the cabinet and pulled out several jars, not with his usual care, but with a clattering fury. He slammed a heavy mortar and pestle down on his work table, dumping the contents of the jars into the bowl—dried roots, dark powders, crushed minerals. He gripped the pestle and began to smash the items into a fine powder, his movements angry and violent, the grinding of the stone a counterpoint to the music from above.

He picked up the bowl and poured the gray, gritty powder into his right hand, cupping it tightly. He strode out of the conjure room and moved to the front door.

"Where you going, Obie?" Lizzie called out from the kitchen.

He didn't answer. He was out in the hall and flying up the steps, taking them two at a time. He reached the Jeffersons' door and knocked, not with two polite taps, but with three loud, insistent bangs that echoed in the stairwell.

He stood there, listening to the piano play on for a moment. Then it stopped.

The door opened to reveal Chantelle, a look of surprise on her face.

Chantelle opened the door. He stood there, his hands clasped politely behind his back.

"Good afternoon," Roddie said, his voice a low, almost predatory calm. He took a half-step forward, crossing the threshold into their apartment. "I am Dr. Obie Roddie. I live downstairs. The music… it's a bit too loud."

Chantelle was confused by his formal tone, his unassuming presence. Before she could say anything, he smiled, thinking he was being sneaky. While her eyes were on his face, he subtly opened the fist he held behind his back. The fine gray powder sifted from his fingers, falling silently in a small heap just inside their door.

Suddenly, Alberta appeared from the sitting room. "What do you want?" she demanded. Her eyes darted down and saw the powder he was sprinkling onto her floor. She came unglued.

Alex, hearing the commotion, walked slowly to the door, his face pale but his expression firm. Seeing her husband near the intruder, Alberta shoved Roddie.

"You get out!" she shrieked, her voice cracking with rage and terror. "Get out now, you devil!" Roddie's face darkened, his own anger rising to meet hers. "God will strike you down!" she screamed.

Chantelle grabbed her aunt's arm. "Auntie, please!"

Alex, who was always friendly, who had always offered a kind word, moved closer to the door, his eyes filled with a quiet, steely determination Roddie had never seen before. "Son," he said, his voice low but unwavering. "You best get going. You aren't welcome here."

Roddie stood there, his hand now empty, his fury momentarily checked by the unified front before him. He saw the resolve in Alex's eyes, the fear in Chantelle's, the righteous hatred in Alberta's. He shook his head in disgust and slowly, deliberately, turned and went back downstairs.

His own apartment door was open. Lizzie was standing there, her arms crossed, her face a mask of anger and disappointment.

"What were you doing, Obie?" she said, her voice tight. "Leave them alone."

He was so mad he stormed right past her without a word, disappearing behind the beaded curtain. Roddie went to a locked cabinet, opened it, and pulled out his black notebook. He slammed it on the table and quickly flipped through the pages. When Roddie found the page he was looking for, he began chanting loudly, filling the small apartment with ancient, powerful words.

Lizzie stormed in after him. "Damnit, Roddie! Enough!"

He kept chanting, his eyes closed, ignoring her completely. He was lost to her, lost to everything but his rage and his work.

Defeated, she turned and walked back into the bedroom, slamming the door behind her. But the sound was swallowed whole by the power of his chanting voice.

♦♦♦♦♦♦

Back in the apartment, Alberta was coming unglued. She paced the sitting room like a caged animal, her hands twisting the fabric of her dress.

"He came into our home, Alex! He dropped his evil right on our floor!"

"Bertie, please, sit down," Alex pleaded from his armchair, his voice weak.

Chantelle rushed to her side with a glass of water. "Auntie, please. Drink this."

Alberta ignored them both. She stood abruptly and marched to the hall closet, retrieving the broom. With a look of grim determination, she swept the small gray pile of powder Roddie had left out of her apartment and into the hallway. But she didn't stop there. With big, flowing, furious sweeps, she began to cleanse the entire hallway, knocking dust and debris down the corridor in a thick cloud.

"Evil be gone!" she shouted, her voice echoing in

the stairwell. "In the name of the Lord, be GONE!"

From their doorway, Alex and Chantelle exchanged a look of deep and profound worry.

Alberta came back inside, her breath ragged and slammed the broom back into the closet. Her frantic energy was gone, replaced by a sudden, unnerving calm. "I'm going to the church," she announced. "I need to see the reverend."

She grabbed her purse and walked out, pulling the door firmly shut behind her. Her footsteps were heavy and deliberate on the stairs. When she reached the second-floor landing, she paused. She turned and stared down the short, dim hallway at the door to apartment 203. It was just a door, plain and silent, but to Alberta, it was the gate to a pit, a place where evil breathed and plotted. After a long, hard moment, she turned away and continued her descent.

Outside, the afternoon sun was bright. The normal sounds of Knoxville filled the air—a trolley clattering past, the murmur of conversation from a nearby storefront. Alberta noticed none of it. She walked the few blocks to the church with a singular, burning purpose, her eyes fixed forward, her mind a world away from the everyday lives of the people she passed.

The heavy oak doors of First Baptist Church were open. She found Reverend Thompson in his study, surrounded by stacks of books, a large Bible open on his desk as he prepared his next sermon. He looked up as she entered, his kind face creasing with concern.

"Alberta. Please, come in. Sit down."

She did, and the story poured out of her—the piano, the arguments, the powder at the door, Alex's heart attack, the fire that killed Mr. Gable, the dismissals from the doctor and the police. She told him everything.

The reverend listened patiently, his hands steepled, his expression thoughtful. He did not laugh or smirk. He nodded slowly, acknowledging the weight of her terror. When she was finished, he picked up his Bible and thumbed through its thin, worn pages, his eyes scanning the text.

"The spiritual world is real, Alberta," he said, his voice a low, comforting rumble. "And the Word tells us that our true battle is not what it often appears to be." His finger stopped on a page in the book of Ephesians. He looked up at her.

"It says, 'we wrestle not against flesh and blood, but against principalities, against powers, against the rulers of the darkness of this world.'" He leaned forward, his expression earnest. "Do you see? Your fight is not with a man. It is with the spiritual wickedness that commands him."

"But what do I do, Reverend?" she pleaded. "How do I fight it?"

"The Word tells us," he said, his voice gaining strength. "It says to 'put on the whole armor of God, that ye may be able to stand against the wiles of the devil.' It does not say we must raise our own hand, Alberta. It says we must stand, armed with righteousness as our breastplate, and truth." He tapped the Bible with his finger.

"'Above all,' it says, you must take up the 'shield of faith,' to quench all the fiery darts of the wicked. And you must take the 'sword of the Spirit,' which is the word of God." He closed the Bible gently.

"The battle is won through prayer, Alberta. By 'praying always with all prayer and supplication in the

Spirit.' That is the task before you." He sighed, seeing the desperate, unsatisfied look in her eyes. "This is a heavy burden you carry. I will pray for guidance. For you and for your husband."

Alberta looked at the good, kind man before her. He believed her, but he couldn't help her. Not in the way she needed. He offered her prayer and scripture, but she needed a weapon against a man who had declared war. She left the church feeling more unsatisfied, more determined, and more emotionally isolated than ever before. The final door had closed. If God needed a hand to smite the evil in her building, she decided, it would have to be her own.

♦♦♦♦♦♦

The chanting had been going on for almost two hours.

From her place in the kitchen, Lizzie Roddie could hear the low, resonant drone of her husband's voice from behind the beaded curtain of the conjure room. It was a sound she usually found comforting, the familiar rhythm of his work. But not anymore. Now, it sounded menacing, obsessive. The words Alberta Jefferson had shrieked at her on the landing—*Your husband did this!*—played in her mind on a loop.

Lizzie stood, her hands trembling slightly. She couldn't sit still any longer. She had to do something.

As she walked to her front door, Obie's chanting continued, unabated. She slipped out into the hallway and climbed the single flight of stairs, each step heavy with dread. She knocked softly on the Jeffersons' door.

A moment later, it opened. Alex stood there, his

face pale and drawn. He looked surprised to see her.

"Mrs. Roddie?"

"Mr. Jefferson," she began, her voice barely a whisper. "I am so sorry to bother you. I just... I had to come and see how you were feeling. And to apologize."

He looked at her, his kind eyes searching her face. "Apologize for what?"

"For the conflict between our families," she said, tears welling in her eyes. "For my husband's temper. For being such poor neighbors. I am so, so sorry that you've taken ill."

Seeing the genuine distress on her face, Alex's expression softened. "Thank you, Mrs. Roddie. That's... that's kind of you. Tensions have been high for everyone."

"Please, get well," she whispered, knowing there was nothing more she could say. She turned to leave, feeling a small, fragile sense of relief.

Just as Lizzie stepped out into the hallway, Alberta was coming up the final stair. The two women froze, locking eyes across the landing.

Alberta's face, which had been set in weary determination, hardened instantly into a mask of cold fury. She saw the wife of her tormentor leaving her apartment, having just had a secret meeting with her vulnerable husband. All of her worst fears and deepest suspicions were confirmed in that single, silent moment.

Seeing the look on Alberta's face, Lizzie's heart sank. Her well-intentioned visit had been a catastrophic mistake. Without another word, she scurried down the stairs, the sound of her own hurried footsteps echoing in the quiet hall. Alberta watched her go, then turned and entered her apartment.

As she stepped into the sitting room she was met with a smell so comforting and familiar it almost brought her to her knees: roast beef and onions. The warm, savory scent was a stark contrast to the cold dread that had settled in her heart.

Alex was standing in the doorway of the kitchen, leaning against the frame for support. "There you are," he said softly.

Alberta's face was a mask of fury. "What was that woman doing in our home?" she demanded, her voice low and sharp.

"Bertie, now, calm down, honey…" Alex started, taken aback by her tone.

"No!" she snapped, her voice rising. "Her husband is evil! Did you let her in here, Alex?"

Chantelle came running in from the kitchen, wiping her hands on her apron. "Auntie Bertie, what is it? Please, calm down."

"She came to apologize," Alex explained, trying to disarm the situation. "She was worried about me. She wants peace, Bertie, just like I do."

Alberta stared at him, her chest heaving, the argument still raging in her eyes. Alex, seeing the fight in her, simply opened his arms. "Come here," he said gently.

She looked from her weakened husband to her worried niece, and the rigid anger in her spine finally gave way to a wave of utter exhaustion. She slowly walked into his embrace and melted against him, her head resting on his chest. For a few precious moments, she felt safe.

Chantelle piped up from the doorway, breaking the tense silence. "Auntie Alberta, I made a roast. Are you hungry?"

Alberta pulled away from Alex, a real hunger pang reminding her she hadn't eaten since breakfast. "Yes, child," she said, her voice thick with emotion. "I am."

They sat down at the small kitchen table, the platter of sliced roast beef and potatoes steaming between them. Alex reached out and took his wife's hand, then Chantelle's. He bowed his head.

"Lord," he began, his voice a little weak but clear as a bell. "We ask you to bless this place and our family. Please watch over us, grant us peace in these trying times, and…" he paused, peeking at the platter of food, a familiar twinkle returning to his eyes, "…thank you, Lord, for this big ol' roast in front of us! Amen."

Chantelle let out a giggle. Alex grinned. Alberta looked at her husband, at his unshakeable humor shining through the sickness and fear, and a real, honest laugh escaped her lips. It felt foreign and wonderful. As they passed the plates and filled their forks, the mood was lighter than it had been in weeks. For a moment, sitting at the table, they were just a family again, and the devil downstairs felt very, very far away.

♦♦♦♦♦♦

The chanting filled the small apartment, a low, resonant drone of anger and power. The beaded curtain to the conjure room flew open, clattering loudly as Lizzie stormed in.

"Enough!" she shouted over the sound of his voice. "Stop!"

Roddie stopped mid-chant, his head snapping up. His eyes were dark with fury but also surprise at her forceful tone.

"What in the world are you even chanting for, Obie?" she demanded, her hands on her hips.

His voice was a low growl. "Retribution. A reckoning."

"All this anger isn't getting us anywhere," she said, her voice firm. "It's just making things worse. Why don't we go talk to Felix tomorrow morning? See if we can get out of our contract. Let's find something bigger, a proper house. Your business is going well, isn't it?"

Roddie gave a curt, almost imperceptible nod.

"Then let's leave this place and all its trouble behind," she pleaded. She took a breath, her expression softening. "I… I just spoke to Mr. Jefferson upstairs."

Roddie's head shot up. "What?"

"He doesn't want conflict, Obie," she said sheepishly. "He's actually a very kind man. He seems tired, is all. Perhaps you should go speak to him. Man to man. Maybe… maybe even invite him and his wife over for supper. I'll make them anything they want if it will just calm things down."

The anger in Roddie's face seemed to drain away, replaced by a deep, weary sorrow. He ran a hand over his face, the fight going out of him. "You are right," he said quietly. "I am sorry. The music… I just let it get to me." He looked at her, his eyes pleading for her to understand. "But you have to understand, Lizzie. When I'm with a client, I must concentrate. I have to focus all my energy on them, on their need. That damn piano upstairs… it makes it so hard to do my work."

There was a long pause, the silence in the room now feeling heavy with unspoken words.

"But I will try to do better," he finally said.

"Perhaps I will talk to him." He looked down at the black notebook on the table. "If you will, please give me a few more moments."

Lizzie pulled her hair up, her relief palpable. "Fine," she said softly. "I'm going to start getting ready for bed."

She slipped back through the beaded curtain. Roddie watched her go, then a faint, thoughtful smile touched his lips. He picked up the notebook from the corner of the table and began to flip slowly through the pages until he came to one titled **MISFORTUNE**. He rubbed his chin slowly and began to read.

♦♦♦♦♦♦

That night, Glenda's house felt heavy with the ghost of Willis's anger and the sharp, lingering scent of her own heartbreak. She was sitting on the couch in the dark, a cold washcloth pressed to her throbbing cheek, when a knock came at the door.

Delphine let herself in, her face a mask of grim determination. She held a small, folded slip of paper in her hand.

"What are you doing here, Della?" Glenda asked, her voice hoarse from crying.

Delphine walked over and sat beside her sister on the couch, her expression a mixture of pity and grim determination. "I want to help fix things," she said softly but firmly.

"There's nothing left to fix."

"I went back to see Dr. Roddie," Delphine said, her voice low and urgent as she sat beside her sister.

Glenda recoiled. "You want me to go back to Willis? After what happened? Look at my face, Della!"

"He didn't mean for this to happen," Delphine insisted. "Dr. Roddie says you and Willis are cursed. Someone put something on you both to make everything go wrong."

"Cursed?" Glenda laughed, a bitter, broken sound. "I'm not cursed, I was a fool. A fool to listen to you, and a fool to ever trust a man like Willis Greene."

"This will break it," Delphine said, unfolding the paper with Roddie's instructions. "This will fix it. Now, fetch me a handkerchief."

"No," Glenda said, shaking her head. "No more of this foolishness."

"This is different," her sister pleaded, her eyes shining with a desperate faith. "This isn't to make someone love you. This is to take the evil off you. Please, Glenda. What else can we do?"

Finally, worn down by her own grief, Glenda stood and retrieved one of their father's old cotton handkerchiefs from a dresser drawer. With a sigh, she handed it to Delphine.

As instructed, Delphine tied three tight, hard knots in the center of the cloth. She went to the kitchen and filled a small bowl with the murky dishwater left over from supper, a few flecks of food still swirling in the gray water. She brought it back to the sitting room.

"Dip it," she commanded softly.

Glenda shuddered, but she took the knotted handkerchief and submerged it in the dirty water, holding it there until it was completely saturated. She pulled it out, dripping and soiled.

"Now we let it dry," Delphine said, placing it carefully on the kitchen windowsill. "And once it's dry, you are to carry it in your pocket at all times. It will repel whatever evil has taken root in your lives. It will make things right."

Glenda couldn't help but roll her eyes.

"Just wait, this will work." Delphine said. "I believe it."

It Is Well with My Soul

The next morning, for the first time in weeks, Alberta slept in. She was woken not by a nightmare or the jolt of anxiety, but by the gentle, familiar sound of the piano. Alex was playing "It Is Well with My Soul," the chords full and resonant, filled with a peaceful confidence she hadn't heard in ages. She found herself humming along from her bed, a real, hopeful smile spreading across her face as she rose.

She walked quietly into the sitting room and saw him there, his back to her, his shoulders relaxed as his fingers moved across the keys. She watched him from the doorway, softly singing the words to herself, a wave of profound relief washing over her. The worst was over.

After a moment, she walked over and placed a hand on his shoulder. He turned to her, beaming. "Morning, darling."

But as he smiled, she noticed it. A small, glistening bead of red at the edge of his nostril. It was so tiny she almost didn't register it. She stopped singing, her brow furrowing in confusion. He didn't seem to notice. He turned back to the piano to begin the next verse.

As his hands came down, a single, perfect drop of crimson fell from his nose and landed silently on a pristine white key.

The beautiful hymn stopped with a discordant clunk. Alex's hands flew to his face. When he pulled them away, his fingers were smeared with blood. Another drop fell, then another. The blood was coming faster now.

Alberta's confusion evaporated, replaced by a pure, clarifying rage.

"It's him!" she began to scream, her voice a raw tear in the fabric of the morning. "It's him! That devil downstairs did this!"

As Alex stumbled from the piano bench and rushed to the bathroom, clutching his bleeding nose, Alberta ran in the opposite direction. She flew into their bedroom and yanked open the drawer of her nightstand. Her hand closed around the cold, heavy steel of a revolver.

She turned and strode purposefully toward the front door, her face a mask of terrible resolve.

"Bertie!" Alex's panicked voice called out from the bathroom. "Where are you going?! Bertie, what are you doing!"

Roddie sat at the table in his conjure room, hunched over his notebook. He stared at the page, but he wasn't reading.

A loud knock echoed from the front door.

Lizzie moved down the hall from the kitchen to answer it, but Roddie jumped up from his chair. "I got it," he called out.

He stood at the door for a long moment, composing himself. He slowly pulled the door open.

Stanley Carr stood on the welcome mat, beaming, his face transformed from the tired, downtrodden man Roddie had met just days before.

"Dr. Roddie!"

Roddie was surprised to see him. "Good morning, Mr. Carr. It's nice to see you, sir."

"Doctor, I had to come tell you the good news!" Stanley said, his voice brimming with excitement. "Everything you told me to do! It worked! I got promoted!"

Roddie was pleasantly surprised. "That is wonderful news, Mr. Carr."

"Yes, it all happened so quickly," Stanley continued, practically bouncing on the balls of his feet. "Willis, the guy they just promoted, got fired for being drunk on the job! And the plant manager, he immediately offered me the supervisor position at the mill!"

Stanley was on cloud nine, but Roddie's mind was racing, a cold dread washing over him. He stared at Stanley, his face a blank mask. There was a long silence.

Finally, he spoke, his voice quiet. "You said… Willis?"

Stanley nodded slowly, not understanding the shift in the doctor's demeanor. "Yes, he they let him go."

Roddie paused again, the pieces clicking into place with horrifying clarity. "Willis Greene?"

Stanley was puzzled. "Yes. Do you know him?"

The name hit Roddie like a ton of bricks. The hex for Stanley Carr and the blessing for Delphine Tucker's sister had landed on the same man. He took an involuntary step back, leaning against the door frame for support as the tangled consequences of his work revealed themselves. "I'm afraid Mr. Greene and I haven't met," he said, his voice hollow. He didn't know what else to say.

Stanley was confused by the doctor's strange reaction, but he was too happy to dwell on it. He reached into his back pocket and pulled out his wallet. "Doctor, I just wanted to come by and thank you properly." He pulled out two crisp twenty-dollar bills. "You asked me to come by and pay you twenty dollars when I got promoted. Well, here's forty."

He extended the money to Roddie. Roddie hesitated, then took the bills with a weak, trembling smile. "Thank you, Mr. Carr."

"Okay, I need to get going," Stanley said cheerfully. "I don't want to be late now that I'm the supervisor!"

As soon as he turned around, he stopped dead in his tracks. Alberta Jefferson was walking slowly down the stairs behind him, her face calm and resolute, a heavy revolver held firmly in her right hand.

Stanley's eyes widened in terror. He scrambled out of the way, pressing himself against the wall of the stairwell as she reached the landing.

She stopped in front of the open doorway. In her hurry, her movements were no longer slow, but filled with a terrible, swift purpose. She raised the gun, leveling it at Dr. Roddie's shocked face.

From the stairwell, Stanley saw her finger tighten on the trigger and he cried out, his voice a desperate crack in the tense silence. "Ma'am, no!"

The sudden shout from behind her made Alberta flinch. Her body convulsed in surprise, and in that instant, her finger jerked the trigger.

The shot was deafening. The bullet slammed into Roddie's chest, throwing him back a step. He let out a sharp grunt of pain and shock, his hands flying to the wound. He doubled over, stumbling against the door frame, but did not fall. He looked up, his eyes wide with disbelief and agony.

Stanley quickly fled down the stairwell.

From the back of the apartment, Lizzie screamed, "Obie!" and appeared in the doorway behind her husband, her face a mask of pure horror.

Roddie ignored her. His gaze was locked on Alberta. Through a bloody cough, he managed to rasp, his voice a low, venomous whisper, "A hex… upon you."

Alberta's face was like stone. She stepped forward, stepping into the doorway. She pressed the hot barrel of the revolver against his forehead. Lizzie screamed, "No!"

She pulled the trigger.

The second shot was muffled and absolute. Roddie's body went limp and dropped like a sack of potatoes, his lifeless form crumpling in the doorway as blood splattered across Alberta's dress, the wall beside him, and the horrified face of his wife, who stood frozen just a few feet away.

A piercing, inhuman wail came from Lizzie. She rushed forward and fell to her knees, cradling her husband's bloody, lifeless body. The crimson soaked instantly into her light blue dress as she sobbed and screamed for help.

Alberta lowered the gun. She calmly turned and walked back upstairs.

Alex was at their apartment door, holding a white rag soaked with dark spots of blood to his nose. "Bertie?" he asked, his voice shaking. "What's going on? What did you do?"

With a look of serene satisfaction, she walked past him. She set the gun gently on the coffee table and sat on the couch, folding her hands in her lap and staring straight ahead with a wide, radiant grin on her face.

♦♦♦♦♦♦

Felix Acres rushed up the stairs as quickly as his old legs could carry him, drawn by the sound of gunshots and Lizzie's piercing screams. When he reached the second-floor landing and saw Dr. Roddie's body crumpled in the doorway, he gasped, "Oh, no. Lord have mercy." Other neighbors were peeking out of their doors now, their faces a mixture of fear and morbid curiosity. Leaving the hysterical, sobbing Lizzie, Felix turned and hurried back to his small first-floor apartment, his hand shaking as he picked up the receiver of his black rotary phone.

A few minutes later, the heavy, authoritative footsteps of the police echoed in the stairwell. Officer Miller was one of the first on the scene, his face grim as he took in the bloody scene on the landing.

Lizzie, her light blue dress now stained a horrific, dark crimson, looked up at him with wild eyes. "It was her," she sobbed, pointing a trembling finger up the stairs. "The woman upstairs. Mrs. Jefferson."

The police huddled for a moment. Then, Miller and two other officers took the stairs, their hands resting on their holsters. Miller found the Jeffersons' apartment door ajar. He knocked once before pushing it open.

The scene inside was eerily calm. Alberta Jefferson sat perfectly composed on her couch, her hands folded in her lap. Next to her, a frazzled Alex stared at her, a bloody rag still clutched in his hand. The revolver sat on the coffee table.

Officer Miller's eyes met Alberta's. He recognized her immediately.

She looked up at him and offered a small, serene smile. "I told you," she said, her voice even. "He put a hex on my husband. Tried to kill him. Nobody would do anything, so I had to take matters into my own hands."

"Ma'am," Miller said flatly. "I'm going to have to ask you to come with me down to the station. We need to ask you some questions."

She nodded once, a gesture of polite agreement. "Of course." She slowly stood. She offered no resistance, no fight at all. As Miller pulled out his handcuffs, she let out a soft laugh.

"Honey," she said, almost pityingly. "You don't need those. I'll go with you."

Miller hesitated, then gave a slight shrug to his partner. They walked her to the door.

As they escorted her downstairs, she paused on the second-floor landing. Lizzie was standing now, talking to another officer, her body shaking. A white sheet had been placed over Roddie's body, but two dark red stains were already seeping through the fabric. For a moment, a look of remorse flickered in Alberta's eyes—not for Roddie, but for the weeping woman before her.

"Honey," Alberta said softly, her voice carrying across the landing. "I wish there had been another way."

Lizzie just stared back, speechless, her face a mask of incomprehensible grief.

Officer Miller gave Alberta a gentle nudge. "Come along, Mrs. Jefferson."

As they reached the front entrance, an ambulance was arriving. Two men emerged with a gurney to take the body away. The hallway was alive now with the whispers and murmurs of the other tenants, the story of the voodoo doctor and the piano teacher's wife already beginning to curdle into legend.

♦♦♦♦♦♦

Later that night, the sounds of the police station were a low, steady hum outside the bars of the holding cell. Typewriters clacked, phones rang in the distance, and the low murmur of men's voices drifted down the hall. Alberta Jefferson sat on the edge of a narrow cot, her back straight, her hands folded in her lap. She was not scared. She was patient.

Footsteps approached, and Officer Miller appeared at the cell door, a man in a wrinkled suit standing beside him.

"Mrs. Jefferson," Miller said, his tone tired but professional. "This is Richard Bell. He's a public defender."

Mr. Bell, a man with a kind, weary face, smiled gently and tipped his hat. "Good evening, ma'am."

Miller unlocked the heavy door, the sound of the bolt sliding back echoing in the quiet hall. Bell stepped inside as the officer remained by the door. "I've just been made aware of your case, Mrs. Jefferson," the lawyer began, taking a small notepad from his coat pocket. "Can I go over the details with you? I was told the deceased… Mr. Roddie… tried to harm your husband?"

Alberta nodded her head emphatically, her eyes lighting up with a fire of conviction. "He sure did!"

"Can you tell me what happened?"

She told him everything. She spoke of the strange, gray powder left in a line at her door, and how it had made her violently ill. She told him about her husband's first collapse and his trip to the hospital. She described how Roddie had brazenly come inside their home just a day ago and dropped another powder on their floor, and how, ten hours later, her husband's nose began to bleed so badly she thought he might die.

Bell sat on the edge of the cot beside her, listening intently and jotting down notes. He was quiet for a long time after she finished, his brow furrowed in thought.

Finally, he looked at her. "Mrs. Jefferson," he said slowly, "from what you're telling me, it sounds like self-defense to me. This man was openly trying to harm you. It's unfortunate, but you did what you had to do to protect your family."

A wave of relief washed over Alberta. For the first time, someone in a position of authority was listening, believing. "Exactly!" she said, her voice full of vindication.

The lawyer's expression grew grave. "However, I need to be frank with you. The Attorney General, Hal Clements, has already announced that he wants murder charges. He's going to try to get the death penalty."

The air went out of the small cell.

"Now, I think that's nonsense," Bell continued, his voice low and serious. "I believe it's a clear case of self-defense. At the absolute most, this is manslaughter, which might mean several years in prison. Our job is to make a jury understand the terror you were living under." He stood up and tucked his notepad away.

"For tonight, try to get some rest. We'll talk more in the morning." He paused at the cell door, then looked back at her. "Hope for the best, Mrs. Jefferson. But prepare for the worst."

♦♦♦♦♦♦

The next morning, a sharp, official knock sounded at Lizzie Roddie's door. While he waited, Homicide Detective Carl Bunch's sharp eyes scanned the area, taking in the details. He noticed a few tiny, dark crimson specks on the white wood of the door frame, remnants of the previous day's horror that had been missed in the cleanup.

Lizzie opened the door, her face pale and drawn. She saw the detective wasn't looking at her, but at the frame of the door. Her own eyes followed his gaze. She saw the specks. Her breath caught in her throat. It was her husband's blood. She stared at it, frozen, unable to look away.

The detective, seeing her distress, cleared his throat gently, bringing her back to the present. His expression was grim but sympathetic.

"Ma'am?" he said kindly. "My name is Detective Carl Bunch. I'm with the Knoxville Police Department. I know this is a difficult time, but I need to ask you a few questions."

Lizzie's eyes were swollen, with dark, heavy bags beneath them. She looked as though she hadn't slept at all.

"I'm sorry for your loss, ma'am," the detective began, his voice gentle. "I truly am. But I'm here because I have a job to do. I need to ask you what happened. What you saw."

Lizzie just nodded, stepping back to let him inside.

Detective Bunch walked down the short hallway, his eyes scanning everything.

After a moment, he made his way towards the beaded curtain leading to the conjure room. The air still carried the faint, strange scent of burnt herbs. He gestured toward it. "May I?" She nodded again.

He stepped into the room and stopped, taking in a small altar, the cabinet of jars filled with roots, feathers, and other unidentifiable things. On the table sat a small, black notebook. He picked it up and began to flip through the pages, muttering under his breath.

"What is this? 'Chasing dust'? 'John the Conqueror Root'? 'Witches fire'?"

Lizzie stood in the doorway and said nothing.

Bunch looked up from the notebook, his expression one of professional curiosity now. "How many customers did your husband have, Mrs. Roddie?"

Lizzie went to a drawer in the cabinet and pulled out a simple notepad that served as a ledger, handing it to him. He skimmed the pages, his eyes widening slightly as he did a quick count in his head.

"Wow," he said, letting out a low whistle. "One hundred and seventy-four customers last year. Looks like he was paid just over twenty-one hundred dollars and had another thirteen hundred billed out." He shook his head, unable to hide his surprise at the amount of money.

"He had a lot of clients," Lizzie said quietly. "It was all word of mouth. He helped a lot of people, and word got around town. Seems like every few days there was someone new at the door."

"I'll need to take this notebook with me," Bunch said, tucking it under his arm. She nodded. He halfheartedly poked through a few of the cigar boxes in the cabinet, then turned to the hall.

She led him to the small sitting room and gestured toward a chair. She sat opposite him on the couch, her hands folded tightly in her lap.

"I'm sorry for your loss, ma'am," the detective began again, his voice gentle. "I truly am. But I'm here because I have a job to do. I need to ask you what happened. What you saw."

Lizzie's composure crumbled. "Obie was at the door," she explained, her voice trembling. "He was just talking to a client. I heard… I heard a gunshot, and I ran out. I saw her. Mrs. Jefferson. I saw her fire a second gunshot right into my husband's head." She choked back a sob, her words dissolving into ragged breaths. "So much blood…"

Detective Bunch watched her for a moment, his professional demeanor softening. He closed his notepad. He could see this was all she could handle.

"Okay, Mrs. Roddie," he said gently. "That's enough for today." He stood to leave. "I am very sorry for your loss. If you need anything, or if you remember anything else, please give us a call."

She just nodded, watching as he walked out and closed the door, leaving her alone with the silence.

Holding Dr. Roddie's strange, black notebook in one hand, Detective Bunch climbed the stairs to the third floor. He knocked on the Jefferson's door. It was opened a moment later by their niece, Chantelle. Through the doorway, Bunch could see Alex Jefferson lying on the couch, a pained look on his face.

"Uh, hello," Bunch said, showing his badge. "I'm Detective Bunch from the Knoxville Police Department. I need to speak with you about what happened yesterday."

Alex tried to sit up, but a sharp grimace of pain crossed his face, and he sank back into the cushions.

Chantelle rushed over to him. "Easy, Uncle Alex." She turned back to the detective. "I'm sorry, he's not well."

"It's my arm," Alex explained, his voice strained as he cradled his left arm against his chest. "It really hurts. Almost like it's asleep from the elbow down, but with a burning pain. I don't know what's going on."

"Uh, okay," Bunch said, stepping inside. "Well, sir, if you're up to it, can you tell me what happened yesterday?" He looked from Alex to Chantelle.

"I wasn't here when it happened," Chantelle said quickly, standing protectively near her uncle. "But I know that man downstairs has been very aggressive and hostile towards my aunt and uncle."

Alex nodded wearily. "It all started because I play the piano," he began, his voice tired. "I'm a piano teacher. I have children come in throughout the week for lessons. He... Mr. Roddie... he didn't like to hear it. He told me that he couldn't take care of his patients because of the noise. He wasn't even a real doctor."

Bunch nodded, listening, his pen poised over his notepad.

"A few days ago," Alex continued, "Alberta went outside and found some kind of powder in front of the door. Made her sick right away. A little bit later, I had to go to the hospital. Then, two days ago, he shows up at the door making small talk, and he dropped a handful of something all over the floor, right inside our apartment. The very next morning, my nose starts bleeding so bad it won't stop, and now… now I can't hardly feel my arm." He sighed, the effort of talking wearing him out. "Bertie had been fuming for days, getting more and more scared. But when she saw the blood coming from my nose… she just flew into a rage. I didn't see it happen, Detective. But I know she shot him."

Bunch made a final note and tucked his pad away. A heavy silence filled the room. It was Alex who broke it. "Detective… how is Mrs. Roddie doing?" The question was sincere, filled with a gentle pity.

Bunch shook his head. "Not too good."

Alex grimaced again, this time not from his own pain. "That poor woman… I'd like to go down there and talk to her, but… she probably don't want to see me."

"Yes, sir," Bunch said quietly. "You probably should keep your distance." He stood up, putting his hat back on. "Thank you for your cooperation. We'll be in touch." He paused at the door. "I hope you get to feeling better, sir."

Alex just nodded. Bunch exited, closing the door softly behind him, leaving them in the quiet, heavy air of the apartment.

That afternoon, Detective Bunch walked into the bustling Knoxville police station, looking weary from the day's interviews. He carried Dr. Roddie's black notebook in his hand. Officer Miller, sitting at his desk typing up a report, looked up as he approached.

"What's that?" Miller asked, eyeing the strange-looking book.

Bunch shook his head and tossed the notebook onto Miller's desk. "It's that voodoo doctor's notebook. From the homicide on North Central."

Miller's curiosity was piqued. He picked it up and began to flip through the pages, which were filled with cramped handwriting. A smirk spread across his face as he turned to a page called **PROTECTION** and began to read aloud in a mocking tone.

"Get this, Carl. To protect your home from evil, the book says you make a witch's fire made of old shoes and sulphur.' Then you take the ashes, stir in some black pepper, and scatter it around the yard." He couldn't help but chuckle.

Miller turned another page to one titled **ROMANCE**. "Oh, it gets better. Here's a prescription for a 'lady who can't keep men friends.' She has to wear a special garter on her left leg, with a heart-shaped bag attached." He leaned back in his chair, reading with theatrical flair. "And in that bag, you put 'gold magnetic sand and the blood of the dove.' Can't forget the dove's blood!"

Bunch just rolled his eyes, but Miller was on a roll, flipping to another page titled **LAWSUITS**.

"Okay, last one. This is the recipe for a winning a lawsuit.' Each morning," he said, holding up a finger, "you write down the names of witnesses, the judge, and the opposing lawyer on a piece of paper'" He paused for dramatic effect. "Then, you pour sweet oil over the list and burn it at 9 a.m. Repeat this each day until the trial is over.'"

Miller slapped the desk and roared with laughter. "Can you believe this stuff? People actually paid him for this."

Bunch, looking thoroughly unimpressed, just shook his head and walked away to get a cup of stale coffee.

♦♦♦♦♦♦

That night, Delphine found her sister sitting on the couch, staring out the window at nothing. The anger had gone out of Glenda, leaving behind only a quiet, heavy sadness.

"I know what he did was wrong, Della," Glenda said, her voice hoarse. "But Lord help me, I really do miss him."

Just then, a soft knock came at the door.

Glenda jumped, her eyes wide. She crept to the door and cracked it open just enough to see who was there. She looked back at her sister, her face a mask of shock.

"It's him," she whispered.

A slow, knowing smile spread across Delphine's face. She believed in Dr. Roddie's work.

Glenda opened the door. Willis Greene stood on the landing, looking smaller than she remembered, his hat twisted in his hands. He looked sober and deeply ashamed.

"Glenda," he said, his voice barely audible. "Can...

can I please talk to you?"

Glenda looked to Delphine, her eyes asking a silent question.

"Why don't you go check on the stew," Glenda said with a pointed look. Delphine smiled. "You are right. I'll go check on supper." She picked up a folded newspaper from the coffee table and disappeared into the kitchen.

Willis stepped inside, and Glenda quietly closed the door. He stood awkwardly in the middle of her small parlor, twisting the brim of his hat in his hands, unable to look her in the eye. The silence was heavy, broken only by the ticking of the clock on the mantel.

"Glenda," he began, his voice thick with an emotion she couldn't quite place. "I know I have no right to be here. But I couldn't… I couldn't not try."

She waited, her hand in her apron pocket, her fingers closed around the hard little knot of the handkerchief.

He finally looked at her, and his eyes were red-rimmed and full of a profound shame. "There is no excuse on God's green earth for what I did," he said, his voice cracking. "For raising my hand to you. I see it when I try to sleep. It makes me sick to my stomach, Glenda. The thought of it."

Tears began to stream down his face now, unchecked. "I was so proud of that promotion. I thought… I thought it finally made me the kind of man you deserved. And when Henderson took it away from me, I felt like nothing. Like a fool. I drank because I was a coward, because I couldn't bear to tell you I'd failed you. And I let it turn me into a monster."

He took a shaky step closer. "I can't live without

you. I know I don't deserve you, not after what I did. But I am begging you. Please, Glenda. Be my wife." He was sobbing now, his words tumbling out in a torrent of apology and desperation. "I swear on my mother's grave, a hand will never be raised to you again. I will spend the rest of my life making it up to you, I swear it."

Glenda looked at the man before her, at his brokenness and his raw, undeniable remorse. The fear she had felt was gone, replaced by a strange and sudden clarity. She was touched by his sincerity, by the honest shame in his eyes.

She took him back, not with a rush of passion, but with a quiet, solemn nod. It was a fragile reconciliation, a promise to rebuild something new from the wreckage of what they had been.

In the kitchen, Delphine gave the stew a final stir and turned the heat down to a low simmer. She could hear the quiet, happy murmurs from the other room, and she smiled to herself. She sat at the small kitchen table and absentmindedly flipped through the newspaper, trying to give the couple their privacy as she eavesdropped.

As she turned a page, a headline caught her eye.

HERB DOCTOR SHOT BY WOMAN – DIES

She looked at it intently, her brow furrowed. She scanned the text. *Obie Lee Roddie, 26, of North Central Street… pronounced dead at the scene… police have a suspect in custody…*

Her hand flew to her mouth, stifling a gasp. "Oh, no," she whispered. The paper trembled in her hands. Dr. Roddie… her angel… was dead. She began to cry, quiet, shocked tears at first, which quickly gave way to deep, wrenching sobs.

Glenda and Willis rushed into the kitchen. "Della? What's wrong?"

Delphine couldn't speak. She just pointed a trembling finger at the newspaper on the table. They both leaned over and scanned the headline. Willis looked up, completely confused. But Glenda, staring at the name of the man who had, in his own strange way, just given her back her future, was filled with a profound and complicated sadness.

What Remains

The sky over Old Gray Cemetery was the color of slate, a low, heavy blanket that promised a rain it never delivered. A small, sad group of mourners huddled around a freshly dug grave, their dark clothes stark against the green of the grass.

Lizzie Roddie stood at the edge of the open plot, a black veil covering her face, her hands clasped tightly in front of her. Beside her, Edna Gable was a pillar of silent, steady support. Behind them stood Delphine Tucker, the ever-loyal Stanley Carr in his new suit, and a handful of other faces—the quiet beneficiaries of Roddie's work.

The service was brief, the preacher's words about dust and ashes feeling thin against the vast, gloomy quiet of the cemetery. The sky overhead was a solid, overcast gray. Just as the preacher offered a final "Amen," two figures were seen walking up the path at the bottom of the hill. It was Glenda and Willis Greene. They were holding hands, and even from a distance, they looked happy.

They joined the edge of the small gathering as the simple casket was lowered into the earth. After the mourners began to disperse, Willis approached Stanley Carr, who was standing respectfully by a nearby headstone.

"Stanley," Willis said with a nod.

Stanley, looking confident in his new suit, turned. "Willis. Sorry for your troubles at the mill."

Willis shrugged, a genuine smile on his face. "Don't be. It was the best thing that could have happened. I start at Standard Knitting Mills on Monday.

The pay isn't too bad, AND better hours." He pulled Glenda forward proudly, his arm around her waist. "And much better company. Stanley, I'd like you to meet my fiancée, Glenda."

Glenda beamed, extending her hand. "It's a pleasure to meet you."

Stanley shook her hand. "You as well, ma'am. Congratulations to you both."

The two men, whose fates had been so strangely intertwined by the man they were there to mourn, shared a brief, civil handshake. Willis, happy to show off his new bride-to-be, then guided Glenda over to offer their quiet condolences to the grieving widow.

The casket was lowered into the earth with the rough scrape of straps against wood. When the first shovelful of dirt hit the lid with a hollow thud, Lizzie flinched. One by one, the last few mourners began to approach her, offering a quiet word or a gentle touch on the arm.

Delphine Tucker came forward, her own eyes red from crying. "Oh, Lizzie," she began, her voice thick with emotion. "I just… I had to tell you. Your husband… he was an angel. A blessing to my family." She glanced back at Glenda and Willis, who stood respectfully at a distance. "He saved my sister's relationship. He brought them together."

A faint, sad smile touched Lizzie's lips beneath the veil. It was a small comfort, a confirmation of the good work she always chose to see. "Thank you," she whispered. "That's… kind of you to say."

Stanley Carr stepped up to her other side, his presence steady and confident. He gently placed a supportive arm around her shoulders.

"He was a great man, Mrs. Roddie," Stanley said, his voice full of conviction. "He helped me through a tough time. I am so sorry for your loss."

Lizzie nodded, unable to speak, looking from the grateful faces of his clients to the dark, waiting earth that now held her husband. He was a blessing to some, a devil to another, and she was left standing alone in the middle of it all, under the gloomy, gray sky.

♦♦♦♦♦♦

The hours and days in the city jail holding cell bled into one another, marked only by the shifting light from a high, barred window. Alberta sat on the edge of the narrow cot, reading her Bible, when she heard the sound of footsteps echoing down the concrete hall.

An officer stopped at her cell, the jangle of his keys loud in the quiet. "Mrs. Jefferson, you have visitors."

He slid the heavy bolt back with a deafening clang and swung the door open. Her breath caught in her throat. Her niece, Chantelle, hobbled into the small cell on a pair of wooden crutches, her left leg thick with a plaster cast. Behind her, Alex moved slowly, his own left arm bound tightly in a sling against his chest. He looked pale and ten years older.

"Auntie Alberta," Chantelle said softly, balancing herself on the crutches.

"Chantelle, your leg!" Alberta gasped, rushing forward. "What on earth happened?"

"Oh, it's nothing," Chantelle said, trying to force a smile. "Just a clumsy fool. I took a fall on the stairs at the apartment building. Broke it in two places."

Alberta's eyes shifted to her husband, who leaned

wearily against the bars of the cell door. "And your arm, Alex?"

He wouldn't look her in the eye. He stared down at the floor, his voice tired and heavy. "The doctors… they say there are clots. The medicine they gave me isn't working." He finally looked up, his eyes full of a weary defeat that broke her heart. "They said if it doesn't improve soon, they… they might have to amputate. From the elbow down."

The words hung in the sterile, cold air between them. Alberta stared at her broken family, all of them contained in this tiny, gray cage.

"Bertie," Alex asked softly, "What's your lawyer saying?"

She took a shaky breath. "He says we're going to claim self-defense. That I was protecting my family." Her expression hardened. "But he thinks they're going to try and convict me of murder."

Alberta and her family sat there in silence as her words hung heavy in the air.

A guard's voice, sharp and impersonal, echoed down the hall. "Time's up!"

They all flinched as if struck. The fragile, painful bubble they had created was instantly shattered. Alex leaned forward, his face etched with a pain that had nothing to do with his arm.

"We'll be back as soon as they'll let us, Bertie," he said, his voice a hoarse whisper. "You just… you be strong for me, you hear?"

Tears streamed down Chantelle's face. "We love you so much, Auntie Alberta. We're praying for you every day."

Alberta could only nod, her throat too tight for

words. She watched them stand—Chantelle awkwardly maneuvering her crutches, Alex shuffling weakly on his feet. He turned and gave her one last, heartbreaking look before Chantelle gently guided him away. Alberta stood frozen, watching them slowly, painfully recede down the long, gray corridor until they were out of sight.

She listened until the sound of their shuffling footsteps and the soft thump of the crutches faded completely, replaced by the hollow, indifferent hum of the jail. She was left alone, surrounded by cold concrete and the crushing image of her broken family.

She could hear Roddie's final, venomous whisper as clearly as if he were standing beside her: *A hex… upon you.*

She understood now. Her conviction settled in her soul, heavy and absolute as a tombstone. The jail was not her punishment. It was just the cage he had built to hold her. The curse wasn't just on her; it was on her family. And her real sentence was being forced to sit here, helpless, while the devil from downstairs reached out from beyond the grave to destroy everything she had tried to protect.

♦♦♦♦♦♦

The next day, the walk back from the market was a study in muscle memory. Lizzie's feet knew the cracks in the pavement, her arms knew the weight of the grocery bag. In her mind, she was still calculating portions for two. The habits of a lifetime were hard to break.

As she approached the front entrance of the Riverside Apartments, she saw a familiar figure struggling with the heavy main door. It was the

Jeffersons' niece, Chantelle, her leg in a cast, awkwardly maneuvering a pair of crutches.

For a moment, both women froze. The air in the small space between them grew thick with all the things they could never say to each other. Chantelle looked down, embarrassed. Lizzie's heart ached with a complicated sorrow.

Pushing past the awkwardness, Lizzie stepped forward and pulled the heavy door open, holding it for the younger woman.

Chantelle hobbled through, pausing just inside the hall. She looked at Lizzie, her eyes offering a flicker of gratitude. "Thank you," she said, her voice barely a whisper.

Lizzie managed a small, tight smile in return.

Without another word, Chantelle turned and began the slow, arduous process of navigating the stairs. Lizzie watched her go, the soft *thump-click* of the crutches echoing in the stairwell long after she disappeared from view.

Lizzie entered her own apartment. The silence was absolute. Obie wasn't in the conjure room chanting, he wasn't in the sitting room listening to the radio. His presence, once the force that filled every corner of the home, was now a gaping void. She set the grocery bag on the kitchen table and began to unpack, her movements slow and mechanical.

Her hand closed around a package of his favorite cigarettes. She had bought it without thinking.

That's what finally broke her.

A single, silent tear trailed down her cheek. She walked from the kitchen to the small mantel in the living room and picked up a silver-plated frame. It held a photograph from a few years back—the two of them in a small photography studio downtown, Obie with his arm around her, a wide, easy grin on his face. He looked so happy, so full of life.

She traced the outline of his smiling face with her finger, and the quiet grief she had held at bay with logistics and composure finally gave way. The tears came freely then, hot and silent in the lonely apartment.

The Trial

The doors to the courtroom swung open, and Alberta Jefferson walked in, her public defender, Richard Bell, at her side. The room was a cavern of polished wood and hushed murmurs. Her eyes scanned the gallery and found them. Chantelle was sitting in the second row, her crutches resting beside her. Next to her sat Alex. His left arm was half gone, the sleeve of his coat neatly pinned up at the elbow. The sight of them, so broken, sent a shock through Alberta's heart, and she had to fight back the tears that threatened to fall.

The trial lasted three days. The prosecutor, Jeremiah Majors, painted Alberta as a cold-blooded killer. He argued that she had become obsessed with her neighbor and, in a fit of rage over a petty dispute, had executed him in his own home.

Richard Bell, in turn, argued that this was not a case of murder, but of a terrified woman acting in self-defense against a relentless campaign of psychological and spiritual warfare.

Lizzie Roddie was the prosecution's star witness. When her name was called, a hush fell over the courtroom. She walked to the stand with a slow, fragile grace, a grieving widow in a simple black dress. She kept her eyes downcast as she was sworn in, her voice barely a whisper.

The prosecutor approached her with a look of profound sympathy.

"Mrs. Roddie," he began, his voice soft and paternal. "I know this is incredibly difficult for you. Can you please tell the jury, in your own words, what kind of man your husband, Obie, was?"

Lizzie looked up, dabbing at her eyes with a folded handkerchief. "He was a good man," she said through soft, steady tears. "The kindest man I ever knew. He was gentle. He just... he wanted to help people."

"And his work," Majors continued, gesturing vaguely. "The defense has used some very... colorful language to describe what he did in your home. What would *you* call the work your husband did?"

"He was an herbal doctor," she said firmly, her voice gaining a little strength. "That's all. He used roots, herbs, things from the earth, to help folks with whatever was troubling them."

"So, he wasn't a 'voodoo man' or a 'witch doctor'?"

"No, sir," she said, shaking her head. "He was a healer."

"And did this healer ever express a desire to harm his neighbors, Mr. and Mrs. Jefferson?"

"Never!" Lizzie insisted, her tears returning. "He was... agitated by the piano noise, yes. It was hard for him to concentrate on his work with his patients. But harm them? Obie wouldn't harm a fly. That's not the man he was."

"So, to be perfectly clear for the jury, Mrs. Roddie," Majors concluded, turning slightly to address them. "Your husband was a kind, gentle, herbal doctor who was having a simple dispute with his neighbors over noise?"

"Yes, sir," she whispered. "That's all it was."

"Thank you, Mrs. Roddie. No further questions."

Majors returned to his table, leaving the image of a gentle healer and his grieving widow hanging in the air. Richard Bell waited a moment, then rose from the defense table and approached the witness stand with a gentle, almost sorrowful demeanor.

"Mrs. Roddie," he began, his voice soft. "Isn't it true that your husband was angry about the piano music coming from my client's apartment?"

"He was… agitated by it, yes," Lizzie admitted tearfully.

"And this agitation, it grew over time, did it not? It wasn't just a minor annoyance?"

"He had a lot on his mind," she said evasively.

"So much on his mind, in fact, that the conflict with the Jeffersons had become hostile, isn't that right?"

"I wouldn't say hostile…"

"Then let me ask you this, Mrs. Roddie," Bell said, his voice still gentle but firm. "On the day before your husband's death, did you feel the need to go upstairs to the Jeffersons' apartment to try and make peace?"

Lizzie froze, her hands tightening in her lap. "I… I don't recall."

"You don't recall visiting with Mr. Alex Jefferson in his home before your husband was killed?" Bell pressed, a little louder now. "You don't recall apologizing to him for your husband's temper?"

The prosecutor shouted, "Objection!"

"The witness will answer the question," Judge Bibb said, his voice flat.

Lizzie's composure finally broke. Tears streamed from her eyes. "Yes," she whispered. "I went up there."

"And why did you do that, ma'am?" Bell asked kindly. "Why did you feel the need to go behind your husband's back to apologize to his neighbor?"

"Because the anger… it wasn't getting us anywhere," she sobbed. "I told Mr. Jefferson I was sorry for the conflict… for not being good neighbors."

Bell nodded slowly, letting the weight of her admission settle over the courtroom. He turned to the jury. "A conflict so severe, a temper so frightening, that this good woman felt she had to secretly intervene to try and calm the waters herself." He looked back at Lizzie with sympathy. "Thank you, Mrs. Roddie. I have no further questions."

Stanley Carr was called to the stand next. He walked to the witness box as if he were walking to the gallows, his new suit looking stiff and uncomfortable on his frame. He was visibly nervous, his hands trembling as he was sworn in.

The prosecutor approached him first. "Mr. Carr, you were present at the apartment of Obie Lee Roddie on the morning of April 25th, were you not?"

"Yes, sir," Stanley said quietly.

"And did you witness the defendant, Mrs. Alberta Jefferson, at that location?"

"I did. I was… I was just leaving Mr. Roddie's apartment when she was coming down the stairs."

"And what did you observe, Mr. Carr?"

Stanley swallowed hard, his eyes fixed on a spot on the wall. "She… she had a pistol in her hand. She raised it up and pointed it at Dr. Roddie."

A murmur went through the courtroom.

"What did you do then, sir?" Clements asked.

"I yelled," Stanley said, his voice cracking. "I can't remember what I said. It happened really fast. I tried to stop her."

"And what happened after you yelled?"

"The gun went off," Stanley whispered. "It was so loud. I… I turned and I took off down the stairs as fast as

I could run."

"Thank you, Mr. Carr," Majors said, turning to the jury with a look that said, *See? She was going to shoot him no matter what.* "No further questions."

When Alberta took the stand, she was calm and resolute. She smoothed her simple dress, folded her hands in her lap, and looked directly at her lawyer, Richard Bell.

"Mrs. Jefferson," Bell began, his voice gentle. "Can you please tell the jury, in your own words, how the trouble with your neighbor, Mr. Roddie, began?"

"It started with the piano," Alberta said, her voice clear and steady. "My husband, Alex, is a piano teacher. He gives lessons in our home. The music… it seemed to bother Mr. Roddie."

"And did this bother escalate?"

"Yes, sir," she said. "The day it really got bad, I came home to find a strange powder, like a fine gray powder, laid in a line across our front door. I knew it was from him. I just… I had a feeling deep in my spirit."

"And what happened after you found this powder?" Bell asked.

"I got sick. So terribly sick I couldn't keep a thing down. And then my husband, Alex, who has never had a day of heart trouble in his life, had a heart attack. We had to take him to the hospital."

Bell nodded slowly. "Did Mr. Roddie's aggressions continue after that?"

"Yes," she said, her voice hardening. "The day before… before it happened… he came to our door. He stepped right inside our home, Mr. Bell. And he dropped another handful of that powder right on our floor. Inside our home."

"And what happened the morning of April 25th?"

Alberta's composure finally cracked. A tear traced a path down her cheek, but her voice remained firm. "The next morning, Alex was feeling a little better. He was playing the piano, a hymn. He looked so happy." She paused, taking a shaky breath. "And then... his nose started bleeding. Not a little bit. It was... it was pouring out of him. There was blood on the piano keys, on his shirt... I knew it was the powder. I knew that man was killing him right there in front of my eyes."

"And what did you do then, Mrs. Jefferson?" Bell asked softly.

Alberta's calm demeanor finally began to fracture. Her voice trembled as she spoke. "He put a hex on my husband." Tears welled in her eyes, and she paused, taking a deep, shaky breath to compose herself. The courtroom was utterly silent. After a moment, she looked up, her eyes shining not just with tears but with a fiery, absolute conviction as she stared directly at the jury.

"I saw it with my own eyes," she continued, her voice gaining strength with each word. "I went to the police, and they did nothing. I did what I had to do. I did what any woman would do to protect her family."

Richard Bell let her final words hang in the still air for a long moment, then nodded slowly to the judge. "No further questions."

In his closing argument, Jeremiah Majors strode before the jury, holding Dr. Roddie's black notebook aloft as if it were a cheap novel.

"Mr. Bell would have you believe his client was living in terror of a powerful and evil sorcerer," he began, his voice dripping with sarcasm. "He wants you to believe that this was a case of self-defense against a diabolical campaign of voodoo. Let's look at the work of this so-called 'devil' from downstairs."

He opened the notebook. "If your business is failing, it's best to sprinkle citronella oil, vanilla, wintergreen oil, and dirty mop water with mustard seed around your business doors to revitalize the venture." A few jurors shifted uncomfortably. "For flat feet, his expert advice was to drink a concoction of crushed up flower bulbs, peppermint oil and ice-cold water." He slammed the book shut.

"This is the 'terror' that Mrs. Jefferson claims she was under. Harmless, silly superstition. The truth, ladies and gentlemen, is much simpler. This is a case about a woman who was angry over a petty annoyance and decided to take the law into her own hands. This was not self-defense. This was murder."

Richard Bell rose slowly and walked to the center of the room, his hands empty, his gaze fixed on the jury. His voice was simple and direct.

"Mr. Majors would have you laugh at these strange remedies. And you may," he said quietly. "But for a moment, I ask you to do something much harder. I ask you to imagine what it was like to be Alberta Jefferson. Imagine finding strange powders outside your door and then watching your husband collapse with a heart condition he'd never had. Imagine him getting better, only to have that man come into your home and drop another powder, and then the very next morning, you find your husband bleeding from his nose so badly you think he might die."

He paused, letting the images settle. "Whether you or I believe in curses and hexes is irrelevant today. The evidence has shown that Alberta Jefferson, a devout, god-fearing woman, believed it with every fiber of her being. What matters is that she believed her family was in mortal danger. And she acted on that belief."

Richard Bell let his final words hang in the still air for a long moment, then nodded slowly to the jury and returned to his seat beside Alberta. The courtroom was utterly silent, the air thick with anticipation. All eyes turned to the front of the room.

Judge Fred Bibb cleared his throat, his voice filling the space with solemn authority. "Ladies and gentlemen of the jury," he began, looking at them over the top of his spectacles. "You have now heard all the evidence and the final arguments from both the prosecution and the defense. It is my duty to instruct you on the law as it applies to this case."

He folded his hands on the bench. "The defendant, Mrs. Alberta Jefferson, is charged with murder in the first degree. For you to return a verdict of guilty on this charge, the state must have proven beyond a reasonable doubt that the killing was committed with malice aforethought. This means the act was willful, deliberate, and premeditated. It requires not just the intent to kill, but a period of reflection, however brief, before the act was committed."

He paused, letting them absorb the weight of the charge.

"If you do not find that the evidence supports a charge of murder in the first degree," he continued, "you must then consider the lesser included charge of voluntary manslaughter. Manslaughter is the unlawful killing of another without malice. This occurs if the defendant acted in a sudden heat of passion, or under an extreme emotional disturbance caused by a provocation sufficient to overwhelm the reason of an ordinary person."

His eyes swept across the jurors' faces. "Your task is to weigh the evidence and determine the defendant's state of mind at the time of the act. Was this a calculated, premeditated killing? Or was it the tragic result of a mind that, in that moment, was overcome by what it perceived to be an imminent danger? That is the distinction you must decide."

He gave a final, grave nod. "You may now retire to the jury room to begin your deliberations."

The jury filed out, their faces grim, a heavy silence settling over the courtroom in their wake.

A few hours later when the jury returned, the foreman, a grim-faced man with a large mustache, stood to read the verdict.

"We find the defendant guilty on the charge of voluntary manslaughter."

The foreman continued, "The jury recommends a sentence of no more than three years in the state penitentiary."

Judge Bibb, who had presided over the strange trial with a stern impartiality, accepted the jury's recommendation. "The defendant is hereby sentenced to serve three years in the state penitentiary," he declared, his voice flat. The crack of his gavel was the final, absolute sound in the tense courtroom.

Richard Bell let out a breath he seemed to have been holding for days, a wide, triumphant grin spreading across his face. He grabbed Alberta's arm. "We did it, Alberta! Do you hear me? Voluntary manslaughter! Not murder!"

But Alberta didn't share his enthusiasm.

"We can appeal the conviction!"

She looked at her jubilant lawyer, then her gaze drifted past him to the gallery. She saw Lizzie Roddie slump forward in her seat, her shoulders shaking with what looked like angry, incredulous sobs. Across the aisle, Alex's own shoulders sagged in defeat, and Chantelle, her crutches leaning against the pew beside her, reached out a hand to comfort him. They had avoided the death penalty, but there was no victory in a three-year separation, not with Alex's health so fragile. No one was happy.

A bailiff touched Alberta's elbow gently. "Ma'am."

Alberta stood, her face a mask of calm acceptance. She had been judged by the laws of man, but she knew her war was not over. As she was led away, her eyes met Alex's one last time. She saw his missing arm, Chantelle's crutches, and knew with a chilling certainty that the Dr. Roddie's curse was still at work.

A Prison Within the Prison

A few weeks after the trial, Edna Gable came to visit Alberta. The prison visiting room was a large, cold space that smelled of disinfectant and quiet desperation. Voices echoed off the high ceiling, a low murmur of hushed conversations between inmates and their loved ones at rows of simple tables.

Alberta was led in by a guard and her eyes scanned the room until she saw her old friend waiting at a small table in the corner. She walked over and sat down, her movements slow and weary.

The two women faced each other across the worn wooden table, a heavy silence between them.

"Good afternoon, Alberta," Edna said softly. "I've had you on my mind."

Alberta managed a weak smile. "Edna. Thank you for coming."

"Of course," Edna said, her eyes full of a complicated sympathy. "I wanted to see how you were holding up."

Alberta's smile faded. A weary, defeated sigh escaped her lips, and her hand instinctively went to her temple, rubbing it in a slow circle. "It's these headaches, Edna," she said, her voice low. "I've had one every day since I walked in this place. The aspirin they give you is useless."

Edna's expression was full of a deep, complicated sympathy. "Alberta… I know you don't want to hear it, but he wasn't all evil. Dr. Roddie… he had gifts."

Alberta scoffed. "His gift was ruining my family."

"He knew he was going to die," Edna said quietly.

Alberta stared at her. "What?"

"At the cemetery," Edna continued, her eyes distant with the memory. "For Douglas. Dr. Roddie told me he didn't want to be there in the cemetery. Said he'd be back there soon enough… permanently. He knew, Alberta.

Alberta was stunned into silence, the news creating a crack in her mountain of righteous certainty.

As their time was up, Edna stood. Seeing the pain still etched on her friend's face, she leaned in conspiratorially. "For your headaches," she whispered. "An old friend once told me… try putting a few raw potatoes in each of your shoes. And put the shoes under your bed at night. When you wake up, your headache will be gone."

Alberta raised an eyebrow.

"It can't hurt."

Edna reached across the table and squeezed Alberta's hand. "I'll be praying for you, Alberta. For you and for Alex." Before she turned to go, she leaned over and gave her friend a firm, heartfelt hug. For a moment, Alberta was stiff, but then she relaxed, accepting the comfort.

That evening, the dull, relentless pounding in Alberta's head had become a prison within her prison. The aspirin the infirmary provided was not working. As she walked into the loud, clattering dining hall, the cacophony of scraping trays and loud voices amplified the pain until it was all she could feel. She was ready to try anything. Edna's words, as silly as they sounded, echoed in her mind. *An old friend once told me…*

Her decision made, she moved through the line, her own tray rattling in her trembling hands. At the end of the line, she paused.

"Excuse me," she asked the burly, sweating cook. "Could I possibly have a handful of raw potatoes?" The man stopped ladling gravy and gave her a look of pure disbelief. "What for? You ain't cookin' 'em." "Please," she insisted.

The cook rolled his eyes but wordlessly turned, grabbed four dusty potatoes from a large burlap sack, and dropped them onto her tray with a thud.

Later that night, in the dark and quiet of her cell, Alberta held the potatoes in her hand. They felt cool and solid. Feeling foolish and desperate, she placed two potatoes in each of her shoes and slid them under her narrow cot.

The next morning, she woke slowly. The first thing she noticed was the silence. Not the silence of the prison, but the profound, peaceful quiet inside her own head. For the first time in weeks, the crushing pressure behind her eyes was gone. She sat up, perfectly still, waiting for the familiar throb to return. Nothing. She marveled at the absence of pain, a feeling so foreign it was disorienting.

A jolt of fear shot through her. She scrambled from the cot, dropped to her knees, and pulled the shoes out from underneath. She snatched the potatoes from them and threw them into the small metal trashcan. She stood there in the middle of her cell, breathing heavily, her hand pressed against her chest. The relief she felt was undeniable. *How in the world did that work?*

Before she could even begin to process the implications, the sound of footsteps echoed down the hall, followed by the jangle of keys.

"Jefferson," a guard's voice called out. "You have a visitor."

Alberta's heart leaped, her small miracle of a pain-free morning immediately shattered by a fresh wave of anxiety. A visitor? As she followed the guard down the long, gray corridor, her mind raced. *Could it be Alex? Had Chantelle brought him? Please, Lord, let him be looking better.*

She stepped inside and her heart sank. Alex was thinner, his color poor, his left arm still pinned at the elbow. Chantelle stood beside him without her crutches, but when she stepped forward, she moved with a pronounced, painful-looking limp.

Despite his own condition, Alex's face broke into a relieved smile. "Bertie," he said, rushing forward as best he could to wrap his good arm around her. Chantelle joined the hug, leaning her weight against her aunt for support.

"How are you, honey?" Alex asked, his first thought for her. "Are they treating you alright in here?"

Alberta pulled back, her eyes tracing his arm, then her niece's crooked leg. "Never mind about me," she said, her voice choked with emotion. "Chantelle, your leg…"

Chantelle gave a sad shrug. "It didn't heal right, Auntie. The doctor says I'll always have this limp."

The smile faded from Alex's face, replaced by a weary sadness. "I have some bad news too, Bertie," he said, his voice low. "The circulation… The doctors are worried. They said… they might have to amputate the rest of my arm."

The words hung in the sterile, cold air between them. Alberta stared at her broken family.

Alex, wanting to change the grim subject, looked at her with concern. "What's Mr. Bell saying? Your appeal?"

She took a shaky breath. "It's been denied."

Her words sucked all the air out of the room. For a long time, they just sat together in silence, a fractured family finding what little comfort they could in just being together. They didn't need to say much more; they just enjoyed the company.

A guard's voice, sharp and impersonal, echoed down the hall. "Jefferson. Time's up!"

Alex leaned forward, his face etched with a pain that had nothing to do with his arm. "We'll be back as soon as they'll let us, Bertie," he said, his voice a hoarse whisper. "You just… you be strong for me, you hear?"

Tears streamed down Chantelle's face. "We love you so much, Auntie Alberta. We're praying for you."

Alberta could only nod, her throat too tight for words. She watched them turn—Chantelle with her pained, uneven walk, Alex shuffling weakly beside her. He turned and gave her one last, heartbreaking look before they disappeared down the long, gray corridor.

As the sound of their shuffling footsteps faded, Alberta was led to her cell where she sat alone, the crushing image of her broken family burned into her mind. The silence of the cell pressed in on her. Obie Roddie was dead, but his hex remained, a living poison that was methodically destroying everything she loved.

Her righteous anger was gone, replaced by a cold, terrifying clarity. There was only one person left in the world who might be able to help, who might understand the dark mechanics of what had been unleashed.

She stood and walked to the bars of her cell, her movements calm and deliberate.

"Guard!" she called out, her voice clear and steady.

A moment later, a heavy-set officer appeared. "What is it, Mrs. Jefferson?"

"May I please have a piece of paper and a pencil?" she asked.

The guard, surprised by her polite tone, shrugged and left, returning a minute later with a single sheet of lined paper and a short, sharpened pencil.

Alberta sat at the small metal desk bolted to the wall of her cell. The pencil felt strange and clumsy in her hand. She thought for a long moment, choosing her words with immense care, then began to write.

After she was done, she folded the note neatly and handed it through the bars to the guard. As he walked away with the letter, Alberta sat on the edge of her cot, a new, fragile, and terrifying hope taking root in her heart.

♦♦♦♦♦♦

A few days later, the mail arrived on North Central Street. Lizzie collected the small stack from the floor by the door of her apartment and carried it to the kitchen table. She sifted through the envelopes absently—a bill from the electric company, an advertisement from a downtown department store, and then one that made her pause.

It was a plain white envelope, her name and address written in a neat but unfamiliar hand. There was no return address. A sense of unease settled over her as she took a small paring knife from a drawer and carefully slit it open.

Inside was a single sheet of cheap, lined paper. She unfolded it and began to read.

Dear Mrs. Roddie,

I know I have no right to ask you for anything. I know the pain I have caused you is a debt I can never repay. But I am writing to humbly ask if you would consider coming to visit me. I need to talk to you. Please.

Sincerely,

Alberta Jefferson

Lizzie's eyes widened. She let the paper drift from her fingers onto the table. The request was so audacious, so impossible, that she felt a fresh wave of anger rise in her chest. Visit her? The woman who had murdered her husband?

She stared at the letter, at the polite, carefully formed words. Then, she picked it up and read it again. This time, the anger was replaced by a deep, weary confusion. She saw the desperation behind the humility, the plea buried beneath the polite phrasing.

She set the letter down. The silence of the empty apartment was a heavy weight. She propped her elbow on the table and laid her head on her arm, her gaze fixed on the piece of paper that held an impossible request from the last person on earth she ever expected to hear from again.

♦♦♦♦♦♦

Alberta was sitting on her cot reading her Bible when the guard's footsteps stopped at her cell. "Mrs. Jefferson. You have a visitor."

Alberta's head snapped up, her heart pounding. *She came.* She swallowed hard, her mouth suddenly dry.

She stood, and the guard unlocked the heavy door, leading her down the long, gray corridor. It was a short walk, but it felt like a mile. What do you say to the wife of the man you killed? What words are there for such a thing?

He led her into the visitation room. Lizzie Roddie was sitting at one of the tables, her hands folded neatly in her lap, looking small and uncomfortable. She looked up as Alberta entered, her expression unreadable.

Alberta paused, collecting herself. She took a deep breath and slowly approached the table.

"Is it… is it okay if I sit down?" she asked, her voice barely a whisper.

Lizzie gave a single, curt nod.

Alberta offered a weak, hesitant half-smile and sat opposite her. The silence between them was a heavy, suffocating thing.

"Mrs. Roddie," she began, her voice trembling slightly. "I… I don't really know what to say."

Lizzie didn't chime in. She just waited, her eyes fixed on the surface of the table.

"If I could do it all over again," Alberta continued, fumbling for the words, "I wouldn't have… I hope you believe me when I say I wish it never happened. What I took from you… it's immeasurable. All I can say is that I'm sorry. I am so terribly sorry."

Lizzie looked down at her hands, tears starting to form in her eyes, but she would not let them fall.

"Thank you for coming," Alberta said after a moment. "But… the reason I asked you here is because I need your help."

Lizzie's head lifted, her expression now one of pure confusion. Still, she said nothing.

"Whatever your husband did that morning," Alberta pressed on, her voice gaining a desperate urgency, "it stuck. It burrowed into my family and it will not let go."

Lizzie still didn't know what to say.

"I'm asking you," Alberta said, her voice cracking as she finally broke. "No, I am *begging* you. Can you please undo it? Give my husband and my niece their lives back. Undo whatever your husband did to us." She leaned forward, her own tears now falling freely. "Please!"

Lizzie finally found her words, her voice a shocked whisper. "I don't know how. I don't know how to do the things he did."

"That notebook!" Alberta said, her hope flaring. "The one they had in the courtroom. Maybe if you read it, you could find something. Anything to make my family whole again."

Lizzie shook her head slightly. "I don't have it. The police… they took some things from his office for evidence. His books, his papers… I never got them back."

Alberta's face fell, the hope draining from her as quickly as it had come. "Can you please look into it?" she pleaded, her voice now small and desperate. "My husband is going to lose the rest of his arm. My niece can't walk straight. Please."

A long, weary sigh escaped Lizzie's lips. She looked at the broken woman before her. "I'll… I'll see what I can do."

Alberta smiled softly, a look of profound relief on her face. "Thank you," she whispered. "I suppose that's all I can ask."

Lizzie nodded once, then abruptly stood and

walked to the exit where the guard was standing. She turned back and looked at Alberta, her face a mask of grief and confusion. She tried to smile, but it wasn't really one. Then she turned and left, leaving Alberta to wonder if anything could be done to change her family's misfortune.

♦♦♦♦♦♦

The day after Lizzie's visit, the guard's footsteps stopped at her cell once more.

"Mrs. Jefferson, you have a visitor."

Alberta's heart gave a hopeful leap, thinking perhaps Lizzie had returned with news, but her hope quickly faded when she saw Reverend Bill Thompson walking down the hall, his large Bible clutched in his hand.

The guard let him into the cell, and the reverend took a seat next to her on the narrow cot, the springs groaning under his weight.

"Sister Alberta," he began, his voice a comforting baritone. "I've been praying for you constantly."

"Thank you, Reverend," she said softly.

"I saw Alex and your pretty little niece at church on Sunday," he continued. "They are holding up with such grace. I'm so proud of their strength, despite their health challenges." He patted her hand. "And how have you been holding up in here?"

"I'm healthy enough," she said, her voice dropping. "But I'm stuck in this prison while my family suffers. Reverend, I need you to pray for the hex to be lifted. The one that voodoo man put on us."

Reverend Thompson paused and took a long, deep

breath, his kind face becoming stern. "Sister, that's all hogwash," he said, his voice losing its warmth. "There ain't no such thing as a curse or a hex from a man like that. There is evil in the world, yes, but this voodoo business is silly superstition designed to lead the flock astray. You need to keep your eyes on the Lord."

"But it's real," she insisted, her voice trembling. "I saw what he did."

He got frustrated then, his patience wearing thin. "Sister Alberta, your husband is overweight and getting older. It's only normal for a man his age to have health issues. It's unfortunate, but it's a part of life."

"What about Chantelle?" she pressed. "Her leg?"

He shook his head, dismissing it. "She had an accident. The bone didn't heal right. It's not a curse, Alberta. It's just unfortunate."

She looked at him and saw the wall behind his eyes. He didn't believe her. He wouldn't believe her. The reverend, seeing he had not comforted her, cleared his throat. "May I pray for your family?"

She said yes and bowed her head out of respect, but she did not close her eyes. After he said "Amen", Reverend Thompson began to preach then, his voice filling the small cell with a sermon about faith and forbearance, about trusting in God's mysterious ways and not giving in to fanciful fears. Alberta listened to the words, but they were no longer a comfort. They were just more noise, another door closing in her face.

A Permanent Prison

The three years Alberta Jefferson spent in the Tennessee State Penitentiary were a study in quiet endurance. She was not a troublesome inmate, nor a model one. She was simply a woman doing her time, her fiery conviction having cooled into a hard, dense core of grief.

The years were marked by the occasional, precious visits from her family. She watched from afar as the curse continued its slow work—Alex growing thinner, Chantelle's limp becoming a permanent fixture. She endured it all, a day at a time, until finally, the day came for her to go.

The heavy cell door scraped open, the sound echoing in the quiet morning block. The guard stood in the doorway, his keys jangling from his belt.

"Ready to go home, Mrs. Jefferson?" he asked, his voice a gruff but not unkind rumble.

Alberta looked up from the edge of her cot, and for the first time in three years, a genuine, hopeful smile touched her lips. She gave a single, firm nod.

She stepped out and was led down the long, gray corridor for the last time. She was led to a window where she was handed a stack of release papers.

"Good luck, Mrs. Jefferson," a tired guard said without looking up.

Alberta scribbled her name and then was escorted down another hall where saw the heavy steel door ahead, a sliver of bright, unfamiliar daylight visible underneath it. She couldn't wait to turn the knob and walk out a free woman.

The door groaned open, and she stepped outside. After three years of confinement, the feeling of the sun on her face was a shock, a warmth so foreign it felt like a brand. She took a breath of cool autumn air, thick with the smell of exhaust and damp leaves, and the freedom felt undeserved, a grace she had not earned. She was older, and the righteous fire that had once burned in her eyes had been replaced by a weary, hollowed-out grief.

Across the street, she saw her husband's old Ford. The driver's side door opened, and Alex got out. His left arm was now completely gone, the sleeve of his winter coat pinned neatly to the shoulder. He looked thin and frail, but his face broke into a tearful, joyous smile when he saw her. He waved his good arm high in the air.

"Bertie!" he called out, his voice full of a love that had survived three years of separation and suffering. "Bertie!"

Chantelle emerged from the passenger side, and even from a distance, her permanent, crooked limp was evident as she moved around the car.

For the first time in years, a genuine, unburdened joy filled Alberta's heart. The hex, the prison, the pain—it all vanished once she heard her husband's voice. She ran toward him, tearing down the prison steps and into the street, her eyes locked on his, a radiant smile on her face.

From across the street, she was the most beautiful thing Alex had ever seen. The last three years of pain and loss melted away as he watched his wife run toward him, her face full of the same love he felt. He raised his hand, his heart swelling.

Then, the world dissolved into a blur of motion from the side. The sudden, blaring horn of an automobile. The horrifying screech of tires on asphalt. A police car, moving too fast, swerving too late.

He saw the impact. He saw the way his wife's body was thrown, weightless and broken, onto the cold pavement. The joyful shout of her name choked in his throat and came out as a raw, guttural scream that echoed off the prison walls.

♦♦♦♦♦♦

The next day, Alberta Jefferson lay in a hospital bed, a white sheet pulled up to her chin. She was unconscious, her face peaceful, a stark contrast to the violent chaos of the day before. The room was quiet, filled with the sterile scent of antiseptic.

A doctor spoke in low, somber tones to Alex and Chantelle in the hallway just outside the door. "The impact caused catastrophic damage to her cervical spine," he explained, his voice full of professional pity. "I'm so sorry. She is completely paralyzed. She will have no movement from the neck down."

Alex stared at the doctor, his mind refusing to accept the words. He shook his head in disbelief. Chantelle, her own leg aching in a gesture of phantom sympathy, finally broke, burying her face in her hands as silent, wrenching sobs shook her body.

The curse was complete. Alberta had fought a devil to protect her family, and in doing so, had been delivered to a new, permanent prison. She was a helpless spectator for the rest of her life, trapped in a still body with only her memories and her convictions.

♦♦♦♦♦♦

Meanwhile, over on North Central Street— Lizzie Roddie sat in the conjure room in her apartment, the afternoon light filtering through the lace curtains. On the table sat the old black notebook. She opened it to the first page, a handwritten table of contents, and her finger slowly traced the strange titles of his work—*Infatuation, Retribution, Misfortune...*

Her finger landed on the last one.

REVENGE.

A slow, wide, knowing smile spread across Lizzie's lips.

Author's Note

Thank you for taking this journey into the world of *Hexed*. While the preceding story is a work of historic fiction—with conversations, daily events, and the inner lives of its characters imagined for dramatic purposes—the central, tragic story of Dr. Obie Lee Roddie and Alberta Jefferson is, disturbingly, all too real.

In the late 1940s, a young, 26-year-old voodoo practitioner named Obie Lee Roddie operated a thriving practice out of his apartment on North Central Street in Knoxville, Tennessee. To his many clients, who traveled from as far as Cincinnati and Chattanooga, he was a gifted healer and spiritual advisor, a man who could solve troubles of the heart, of business, or of luck. Many of the strange but specific remedies depicted in this novel, such as placing potatoes in shoes to cure headaches or using a necktie to ensure a lover's faithfulness, are based on his documented practices.

But to his upstairs neighbor, Alberta Jefferson, he was a source of growing terror. The conflict began, just as described, over the constant sound of piano music from the apartment of her husband, Alex, a piano teacher. This simple dispute escalated into a campaign of fear, culminating in Alberta discovering mysterious powders left at her door, which she believed to be a hex intended to harm her family.

The climax of this story is, tragically, not fiction. On April 25, 1948, after a series of provocations left her feeling that her family was in mortal danger, Alberta Jefferson walked down to Dr. Roddie's apartment and shot him to death.

Her subsequent three-day trial captivated Knoxville. Alberta pleaded not guilty, claiming she acted in self-defense against Roddie's voodoo. His widow, Lizzie Roddie, vehemently denied this, insisting her husband was merely a kind "herbal doctor". In the end, the jury, while discounting the voodoo defense, found Alberta guilty of the lesser charge of voluntary manslaughter and sentenced her to three years in prison.

This story remains a haunting piece of local history because it lives at the intersection of faith, fear, and folklore. Was Dr. Roddie a charismatic charlatan whose strange antics pushed a devout woman to madness? Or was he something more?

We may never know. But the final, chilling postscript to the affair is this: while Alberta Jefferson was serving her prison sentence, her five-year-old daughter was struck by a dairy truck and seriously injured —an event many at the time believed to be the ultimate fulfillment of Dr. Roddie's hex.

Made in the USA
Monee, IL
12 July 2025

20801889R00089